EAT LOCAL

Danny King

A Wild Wolf Publication

Published by Wild Wolf Publishing in 2017

First print

ISBN: 978-1-907954-64-1
Also available in E-Book edition

www.wildwolfpublishing.com

*"Because I could not stop for death he kindly stopped for me.
The carriage held but just ourselves – and immortality"*
– Emily Dickinson (1830-86)

For Rod Smith, Jason Flemyng and everyone else who stood out in the cold dark woods in the winter of 2016 and finally brought this story to life. To the cast and crew of *Eat Local*. With thanks.

ALSO BY THE AUTHOR

BOOKS
The Burglar Diaries
The Bank Robber Diaries
The Hitman Diaries
The Pornographer Diaries
Milo's Marauders
Milo's Run
School for Scumbags
Blue Collar
More Burglar Diaries
The Henchmen's Book Club
Infidelity for Beginners
The Executioners
The Monster Man of Horror House
The No.1 Zombie Detective Agency
Dating By Numbers

FILM
The Hitman Diaries (2009) – short
Wild Bill (2012)
Eat Local (2017)
Run Run As Fast As You Can (2017) – short

TELEVISION
Thieves Like Us (2007)

STAGE
The Pornographer Diaries: the play
Killera Dienasgramata (Latvia)

CHAPTER 1

The Fox was hungry.

He hadn't fed for three straight days and the pit in his empty belly compelled him to range further this night, away from the safety of his burrow and into the shadows of winter.

A prolonged cold snap had decimated his diet. All the mice, voles and frogs he normally ate had disappeared, some tucked up underground to wait out the frost while others hadn't been so lucky. But the fox couldn't wait until spring. He was hungry now. He had to feed.

Desperate times called for desperate measures and so the fox found himself pacing the perimeter of the farm before him. Beyond the wire, in the large wooden barns beyond the farmhouse, hundreds of fat succulent chickens roosted in warm straw away from the cold. The fox wasn't greedy. He only wanted one: just one out of the hundreds and hundreds the Thatchers kept for themselves and he would be on his way. Would that be so bad? If he kept quiet, if he snuck in and out with a minimum of disruption, snatched a chicken by the throat and dragged it out into the night, how would they even know he'd been?

The barn was packed to the rafters with poultry so the Thatchers couldn't possibly know how many chickens they had. What difference would one less make?

The fox was a silent killer. He hunted with stealth and with cunning. And he only took what he needed. He usually wanted for nothing, just the right to live, the same as those he shared his territory with.

And yet his neighbours despised him. They laid traps to snare him; searched the hills to gas him out of his burrow; chased him through the woods with packs of dogs to tear him to pieces and blasted him on sight with their shotguns. How many of his kin had he lost that way, their blood daubed across their exultant killers' faces?

Well it wouldn't happen to this fox. He was more cautious than most, more fleet-footed. He would only make his move when he was sure he would not be seen. And as quickly as he had struck, he would sink back into the shadows dragging his supper with him.

And so the fox waited. He waited for Mrs Thatcher to finish swinging her hatchet in the barn. He waited for Mr Thatcher to stop digging his pit in the yard. And he waited for the chickens in the barn to close their eyes and go to sleep.

He waited and watched and readied himself. But just as the Thatchers were about to turn in for the night a set of headlights lit up the farm approach and chased the fox back into the shadows.

The car stopped just short of the farm and Mr Thatcher reappeared at the door. He asked the visitor what he wanted and the visitor told him as succinctly as he could that he required this place for the night. He was seeing some friends and they had arranged to meet here. For most people, stopped short of their beds by a taciturn trespasser, this might have seemed like a strange request but Mr Thatcher didn't seem unduly put out. Indeed he seemed oddly animated at the thought of people – perfect strangers – coming to his farm this evening.

Mr Thatcher asked the visitor who his friends were but the visitor merely shrugged and promised all would be revealed in the fullness of time.

At this point Mrs Thatcher appeared behind her husband, half lurking at his back and half behind the door. She whispered something into her husband's ear and he gave his assent with a wrinkled smile.

The Thatchers now stepped aside and bid the visitor across their threshold. The visitor accepted their kind invitation and squeezed past the two of them. The door closed and a few moments later the lights went out.

The fox continued to watch and wait. He heard several strange sounds but soon all fell quiet. This was the chance he'd been waiting for. This was his moment.

The fox slipped out of the bushes and hurried across the open terrain. The clear starry skies and silvery moon sent his long black shadow chasing across the field behind him. It disappeared the moment he did, beneath the floor of the barn and all at once it was as though he was never there. He could smell his prey on the other side of the planks. He could smell them but they could not sense him. The coop was too crowded, too busy. Their minds were elsewhere. They had no idea of the danger beneath them.

All he needed was a gap in the boards or some rot he could claw his way through but he could find neither. The barn was secure. And so, for the moment, were its inhabitants.

The fox's ears pricked again.

The front door of the farmhouse had opened and someone stepped out. The fox heard footsteps crunching across the gravel courtyard towards where he was skulking and drew too close for comfort. The footsteps stopped next to the barn. The fox held his breath. Slowly, the footsteps began to pace backwards and forwards along the length of the barn until the fox heard a sound that struck him with terror – the cocking of a shotgun.

Forsaking his supper he ran for his life, scurrying out from his hiding place and sprinting across open ground.

He readied himself for the agonising rip of red-hot shot and damned the cold weather for forcing him to take such desperate measures, but to his surprise and great relief no gun blast came.

The fox made it to the treeline but he didn't know how. Finally he dared a backwards glance and saw not the Thatchers as he had expected, but their mysterious guest who had come calling tonight.

The fox couldn't see his eyes as they were shielded behind dark glass, but he had a feeling they could see him, even crouched where he was in the blackness of night.

The man swung the Thatchers' shotgun over his shoulder and started walking the perimeter, glancing in the fox's direction every now and then until a new set of headlights swept across the farm.

The fox had a sneaky feeling that this was not going to be his night. He sank further into the shadows, slipped through the barbed wire fence and decided to try a different approach. He may have been hungry and leaving empty handed but at least he would live to hunt another day.

Which was more than could be said for most of the Thatchers' uninvited guests tonight.

*

The sound of bootsteps running through the brush startled the fox a few moments later. There was someone else out here besides the Thatchers' visitor and he sounded more spooked than the fox.

"Base control, come in, over," the man was saying over and over again, even though there was no one with him to hear. "Base control, I need immediate assistance, over!"

Still there came no response provoking a flurry of expletives that almost singed the fox's ears off.

"Base control, is anyone there, for Christ's sake, over?"

Finally a tinny voice replied into the man's ear as he ran.

"This is base control, identify yourself, over," the voice requested.

"This is 18," the man replied, dispensing with the pleasantries. "I saw it. I acquired our target, over."

The fox wasn't to know but 18 wasn't referring to him. Kitted out as he was in the Special Ops blacks, with silenced sub-machinegun sidearm, night vision goggles, kevlar body armour and combat knife it would've seemed a little heavy handed to take on just a fox. Then again, so did 40 thoroughbred horses, 60 pedigree hounds and as many inbred aristocrats as his Lordship could rustle up and that had never stop anyone before.

So the fox took no risks. He kept his head low, his eyes open and his nose to the wind as he watched 18 run past.

"Is he tracking you now?" the tinny voice asked 18's ear.

"I don't know. Maybe. Probably. I've got to get out of here," 18 replied, thrashing blindly through the foliage in no particular direction.

"Take a deep breath and calm down," the voice suggested. *"Stop where you are count to five."*

"I'd rather not if it's all the same to you," 18 replied, dropping strict military protocol in favour of all out sass.

"Do it now, 18!" the voice insisted, not one to take no for an answer, particularly not from newcomers to the unit.

"Negative sir. He's probably right behind me," 18 insisted.

"Do it now soldier. That's an order. Stop and count to five."

With supreme reluctance 18 stopped running and began instead to count.

"One... two... three..."

"In your head, 18," the voice reminded him. 18 went quiet and mentally ticked off the last two numbers, albeit with a little silent lip-syncing.

"Well? Are you still there?" the voice asked.

18 pinched himself to double check and confirmed, "Yes sir, it seems so".

"Then he's not tracking you," the voice informed him.

"How do you know? How can you tell?" 18 demanded.

"You got to five, didn't you?" the voice pointed out.

Even in the near darkness the fox could see the colour drain from 18's cheeks. That the voice on the other end of the line could've been so cavalier with his life was something the seasoned soldier wouldn't forget. He was a military man through and through, having served with the British army in three different theatres of operations but this was different. This was no mere combat. It was inhuman. Evil incarnate. He had pledged his loyalty to the Colonel when he'd joined his unit. But he hadn't done so just to serve as his canary. Death found all men eventually. But when it came for 18 it was going to have to look a little harder than usual.

"Now here's what I want you to do, 18. I want you to return to where you acquired the target and set up a beacon. We will be with you as soon as we can, but you reacquire our target and this time you don't let it out of your sight. Do you understand? Over."

"Negative sir, I can rendezvous with you at the roadside and walk you back across country to the location. I need back-up to approach the target. Over."

"You're starting to get my back up, 18. Now grow some balls and do your job. Or else you'll have me to contend with it we lose this opportunity. And I'm not a man who takes disappointment on the chin."

18 tried to shake the image of his balls and the Colonel's chin from his mind while he weighed up his options. It was one thing retreating whilst under fire. It was quite another to refuse to enter the fray in the first place.

18 took a deep breath and confirmed, "Understood, Colonel. Over and out."

He turned to head back up the dirt track he'd just sprinted down when a shape darted out in front of him. 18 levelled his SMG and was about to squeeze the trigger when the shape registered with him.

It was a fox. It was just a country fox. And it was staring down the barrel of his gun, caught as he was in the glare of his laser sights.

18 lowered his weapon and breathed a sigh of relief. The fox seemed to sigh with relief too and then a moment later it was gone. The fox went his way and 18 went the other, each shaken and stirred but still in the game.

For the time being.

CHAPTER 2

As Sebastian well knew, all truly great adventures started with a journey, and this weekend's adventure had been no different. He'd caught the Friday night commuter train from London Bridge, changed at East Croydon, changed again at Three Bridges and changed one final time at Horsham before admitting to himself that he had no idea where he was.

He left the train where instructed and took a moment to ponder the sign. It read "Christ's Hospital". Sebastian had never heard of the place but figured it sounded like a pretty good hospital if they could get Jesus back on his feet after all he'd been through.

No other passengers stepped off the packed commuter train – always a sure sign of a thriving metropolis – and with a blast of the station master's whistle and a beep-beep-beep of the doors, the train eased back out of the station to leave Sebastian marooned in deepest darkest Sussex.

"Any boozers near here?" Sebastian asked the Station Master.

"Only me," he replied with a nip of his hip flask before disappearing back into the warmth of his control booth.

Just as he'd feared. Sebastian was no fan of the countryside. He didn't mind it on postcards but in the flesh it was a little too far from the nearest Wetherspoons for his liking.

Fortunately, Sebastian was a man of great resources. He'd bought a four pack of beers at London Bridge and with Churchillian foresight had saved the last can for just such an emergency. On leaving the station he found a convenient kerb on which to perch and reached for his bag. The can was still there, between his change of socks and his spare pants, and it was still acceptably tepid. He plucked the ringpull, sprayed his hand with froth and gave it a loving kiss. Job done.

Sebastian looked at the station clock. It was a little before nine. She'd be here soon. And he couldn't wait.

What a woman Vanessa was. Of that there was no doubt. But what she saw in a mere slip of a lad like Sebastian was open to speculation. Late thirties, divorced, attractive and obviously minted, Vanessa was the very definition of a *femme fatale*, or to use a term that was generally preferred by the lads on Sebastian's cleaning crew, she was a "right saucy *MILF*".

As an orphan, Sebastian had no mother to compare her to, incestuously or otherwise, so perhaps deep down the lads were right and Vanessa appealed to him in a Freudian sense, filling a void he'd carried with him since childhood. Or perhaps it was just because she was minted. Hmm, the more Sebastian thought about it, the more he had to conclude that this was probably the answer.

Sebastian had known only hardship and toil his whole darn life. Born and raised in an orphanage, no one to take care of him, Christmas presents courtesy of the odd charity organisation (when they could afford them) and now a bright future stretching out before him cleaning the toilets of stock brokerage firm in the city, Sebastian was not averse to the idea of a weekend away with a sugar mommy. No one could say he didn't deserve it. Even the lowliest of London's underclasses were due a break every now and again.

Sebastian worked the night shift. When the traders left for the champagne bars of Bishopsgate, Sebastian and his fellow contractors moved in the mop up the 'champagne' they'd sprayed all over the floors of their executive bathrooms. It was grim work but somebody had to do it – and for less than the national minimum wage it seemed — but as Sebastian and his colleagues were often reminded by their supervisor, "If you don't want the job there are ten blokes coming into Dover this very night who do". Mr Kelsey's motivational skills might have left a lot to be desired but he had a point. Beggars could not be choosers, not in this life anyway, and Sebastian was under no allusion as to his long-term career prospects having flunked out of school at 16 (damn grammar), the army at 18 (damn medical), the Prince's Trust at 21 (damn zero tolerance drugs policy) and the music scene at 23 (damn no talent).

Sebastian was now 26. Most of the guys his age were making their marks in life – and all up the walls and over the seats for Sebastian to clean up, it seemed – but Sebastian himself was going nowhere fast. And he knew it.

Working in a brokerage firm had actually appealed to Sebastian. He thought he might glean something as he went along but all he'd gleaned so far was that his life was even shitter than he'd first suspected. The money the 'suited-and-booted' brigade earned was eye-watering, offensive, disgusting even, and yet none of it crumbled Sebastian's way. You might've thought an executive on £25K a month with a £250,000K twice-annual bonus might've left the guy who cleaned his piss up every night the odd £20 tip for a job well done and yet all they ever left was more piss. And shit. And massive toilet paper blockages. It was enough to prompt even the most reasonable of men into voting for Jeremy Corbyn.

But then he met Vanessa. He didn't know what she did but she worked at nights too, to take advantage of the Asian markets she'd said. He never actually saw her at a computer screen or in any of the offices. He'd just pass her in the corridors or occasionally ride up the lift with her. She was one of the few people who ever actually acknowledged Sebastian, and not just to tell him about a skid-mark he'd missed on the outside of the bowl. She was kind, pleasant and very very alluring. She had amazing eyes, almost hypnotically beautiful: the sort of eyes that could see into a person's soul. At least that's how Sebastian felt.

Of course she was way out of his league. In fact Sebastian wasn't even sure they played the same sports. Vanessa was classy, sophisticated and brimming with confidence.

Sebastian was… not.

He was just a puppy to her. A cute little mongrel she could pet as she passed him by and that was all he would ever be. How could he be anything else when every other guy in the place held down six-figure salaries, drove cars that cost five-figures, wore suits that cost four and pissed figures of eight all over the tiles for him to clean up?

And Vanessa went for the big hitters too, mostly the foreign brokers who came over here on short-term contracts, stayed for a merger or two then disappeared into the sun with the fruits of their mouse clicking. How many guys had Sebastian seen

Vanessa step out with during his time here? He didn't know and he wasn't keeping count but enough to conclude she must've been part of the bonus scheme.

But then one night she got talking to Sebastian and not just chit-chatting either but really talking – about life, love and legacies. It was as if she was sounding him out, appraising him, bestowing a confidence upon him even. Sebastian was flattered and flustered all at once but he did his best not to show it. If growing up in an orphanage had taught him anything it was how to mask his true feelings with a pinch of bluff.

"I was thinking about going away this weekend," Vanessa had told him, to which Sebastian replied:

"Me too," which was true, he often thought about going away. He never actually did. No money. But he did think about it a lot.

"Perhaps if your plans fall through you might consider coming with me?" Vanessa had then said.

Sebastian was dumbstruck. Not an unusual state of affairs for him but it was enough for Vanessa to pick up on.

"Of course, if you feel I'm a little too old for you…" she had started to say but Sebastian quickly reassured her on that front.

"You're not old at all. If anything I like 'em a bit older… er…" he said, whilst wondering where his runaway tongue was taking him now.

"Then what?" Vanessa had asked.

"I'm just er… a little bit strapped at the moment," Sebastian had blushed. It was one thing to grab a quick pint after work, quite another to bankroll a whole weekend, especially the sort of weekend Vanessa was probably used to. Vanessa just laughed.

"Oh you silly boy, the room's all paid for. And the food and drink too. What do you think they give us these expense accounts for?"

And so that was it: a weekend of unentitled luxury in the company of an attractive and experienced woman. What more could any self-disrespecting young man ask for? The bogs would still be here when he got back on Monday but for two divine

18

days Sebastian was going to live it up as though they were his last on Earth.

Vanessa had arranged to meet Sebastian at Christ's Hospital at nine. He didn't know why he couldn't drive down with her from London but she insisted she had a few last minute jobs to wrap up first. Besides, the journey had been pleasurable enough. The city had given way to the suburbs just as day had given way to night, then the line had transported Sebastian away from civilisation altogether and into the countryside. He'd not seen a lot of the countryside in his short and sheltered life, just a single coach trip to a working farm when he was a kid. That had smelt funny and was cold, muddy and miserable and it had ruined his best (and only) pair of Adidas. Looking out from the station, it was much the same as he remembered.

Sebastian turned his collar up to stop the chill from nipping his neck and hoped Vanessa would be here soon.

CHAPTER 3

Boniface was on his feet and filibustering before half of his colleagues even had their coats off.

"... You don't need me to tell you this. You all have long memories. You've seen what I've seen. This green and sceptred isle of ours is becoming grey: country estates are being turned into housing estates; national parks into retail parks; grass into glass; bridleways into motorways; and provincial parishes into sprawling urban jungles," he said, pacing his way around the large circular table in the middle of the Thatchers' country kitchen instead of taking a seat like everyone else. He paused for effect and then fixed his eyes on the Duke. "Nine million..."

An audible groan attempted to cut Boniface off in his tracks but he was not to be denied.

"... no no, let me speak. Nine million. That's the total population of my territory and what, what's yours?" he said, once again picking on the Duke from of the throng of frustrated faces now looking up at him.

The Duke wondered how long Boniface had been working on his speech. It didn't sound like an off-the-cuff introduction, especially not his opening gambit about the estates and motorways etc (someone had been thumbing his *Thesaurus* in the weeks leading up to their meeting) but the Duke refused to rise to Boniface's provocation.

"Peter, really? We meet only once every fifty years and you have striven to become a bore," he said, hoping to take the wind out of the younger man's sails but it wasn't to be. Boniface had indeed been working on his patter for the last few weeks and he wasn't about to be deflected from his train of thought just because no one else wanted to hear it.

"Ten million," Boniface said, answering his own question when it became clear the Duke wasn't going to.

"And I cherish each and every one of them," the Duke replied, which was undeniable if a little sardonic.

Somewhere behind Boniface, the old latch door swung open and in stepped the Thatcher's first guest of the evening. Mr

Chen kept his dark glasses on but he set the shotgun down by the door. It was cold outside and the wide open door let in a shock of cold air but no one noticed. Boniface went on pontificating, his colleagues went on shutting him down and the clock went on ticking behind the Duke's level head.

"Twenty minutes," Chen whispered to the Duke, handing him a slip of paper on which he'd scribbled a summery of the call he'd just taken.

"Very good," the Duke replied, sending Chen and his shotgun back out into the cold night's air with a nod towards the door. Boniface had barely taken the exchange in and yet it would prove to have a big impact on this evening's proceedings.

"I'm just stating the facts here," Boniface glowered in a dour Scots brogue that got progressively more dour with every perceived slight.

"As you see them," Alice finally pipped in, irritated that under Coven rules all eight of them had an equal voice and yet here they all were having to listen to the same one over and over again.

"As they are," Boniface countered, glaring at the sweet old lady in front of him as if her hair were made of snakes. "Nine million and ten million," he reminded everyone pointing to himself and the Duke. "Four million, eight million, six million," he continued pointing in turn to Alice, Angel and Thomas in turn.

"Now take away the first two numbers you thought of and add seven," Angel said, much to Boniface's irritation. He could argue the toss all night (and indeed would if need be) but mockery just confused him. Angel knew this was his Achille's heel and enjoyed turning his screws.

"Two and a half million," Boniface said, returning to his pre-prepared text and singling out Henry. "And he doesn't even feed!"

This was more than Henry was prepared to tolerate. He glared back at his accuser and asked: "Is this why you think it's okay to keep poaching on my territory?"

"North of the border's my territory. South of the border's yours."

"Berwick's in England," Henry informed him.

This was news to Boniface. The last time they'd had this disagreement Berwick had been in Scotland. When had it switched?

"Gentlemen, gentlemen, one squabble at a time and I believe I have the rank," the Duke interrupted, finally bringing their proceedings back to some sense of order.

But Boniface still hadn't made his point and he paced the room like a caged beast while most of the others followed him with their eyes. But not Alice. She returned to her knitting. She wasn't really making anything and indeed wasn't much of a knitter. When she was done she would simply have several balls of wool tangled together into a shapeless sheet that she'd throw onto the fire but it was a habit more than anything else. She did it because it gave her something to do with her hands and it helped her blend in. It was part of her look and part of her cover and she'd been doing it for so long now that it had become part of her identity. At least that's how it felt to Alice.

"Sixty million, Duke. Sixty million and counting," Boniface declared. "Yet I remember when the population was just six million. And we were eight then and we're eight now."

"Thinking of breeding are we, Peter?" the Duke smiled, taking a lead from Boniface by asking questions he already knew the answer to.

"Oh no, I'm happy with the friends I've got, thank you very much," Boniface snorted, failing to read the sarcasm in the Duke's tone.

"And so am I," Alice snapped. "But I'd rather not get stuck with you all here tomorrow so get to the point."

Boniface paused for effect and waited for a hushed awe to descend across the room, or as close to it as he was likely to get.

"Quotas," he said, finally naming the elephant in the room.

"Our survey says?" Angel flipped over a piece of paper she'd been holding for most of Boniface's pre-amble. On it was written just one word:
'QUOTAS'.

Henry smirked. The Duke sighed. Thomas groaned. Alice grumbled. And Boniface glowered.

Outside Chen was largely indifferent. He knew the discussion that was taking place without him off by heart. It was the same one they'd had the last time they'd met and the time before that too. In fact, as long as they'd been having these meetings, they'd been having this same argument.

And yet nothing ever changed. So many words. Always the same outcome. Times were changing and yet they were not. Perhaps that was the problem. They were an endangered species. The time had come for them to disappear into the pages of history and yet a few of them continued to cling on – but only just. And only if they followed the rules.

Once upon a time they'd hunted as lions. Now they snuck around like... well, like foxes really, Chen concluded, catching a glimpse of the Thatcher's other trespasser as he sprinted past the barn and ducked into the stable, still hoping to bag a meal tonight.

Chen would've happily opened the chicken coop and let the fox help himself but the fox was too cautious. He'd seen the gun and knew what they could do. He would bide his time. Strike only when it was safe. And live to see his burrow again at dawn.

Chen couldn't blame him for that. He'd been doing much the same thing for the past thousand years and it didn't do to tinker with a winning formula. He wondered why Boniface felt compelled to.

Two hundred yards away, 18 hugged the ground and barely dared to breathe. He lay in a little dip, behind a sprawling oak and bathed in a blanket of night. Not even the moon could see him where he lay but 18 couldn't escape the paranoia that Chen could. He knew what these beings were capable of, despite never having been this close to one before in his life. All his knowledge had come from the endless briefings Mr Larousse had conducted back at basecamp. It had been hard not to smirk at the pious chaplain as he'd lectured them – 40 gruff hairy-arsed ex-special forces veterans – on subjects such as hellfire and immortal demons as if they were all true. Obviously it was nonsense, bogeymen and fairytales for the hard of thinking, but they were prepared to put up with Larousse's twaddle because of what he was paying them. Most private armies would've had to have overthrown a small African nation to secure the sorts of wages Larousse's 'Synod' was offering them. But 18 and his colleagues didn't even have to do anything for it. A few bullshit patrols in the countryside at night, the occasion raid that always came up short and some fire and brimstone Sunday school sermons. It was money for old smoke and nary a shot fired in anger to duck from.

It had all been plain sailing to early retirement for 18 until he'd checked out tonight's target, a Chinese guy who'd gatecrashed a farm. And despite him standing out in the open, just a couple of hundred yards away andwearing a thin jacket and jeans, he showed no heat signal on the thermal image detector at all. Not even his hands. Not even his face. And why the hell was he wearing sunglasses at night?

Oh shit!

It wasn't so much the realisation that their bogeymen existed that got 18 running but his own folly. Because he'd approached tonight's target as he'd approached the last 50, in a less than professional manner. He'd parked up in the lane behind the farm, stamped and trampled his way through the brush and stood in the treeline humming the theme tune to *Star Wars* while he fished out his thermal image finder. Because as far as 18 was concerned, he was just here to take a few pictures of a couple of farmers and tick them off his list. Job done and back to base for cocoa and marshmallows. If he were reconnoitring a training camp in Helmand or a weapons factory in the Sudan then obviously he would've approached his target differently. But this was a farm, in Sussex, manned by a couple of tractor-deaf spud eaters. Exactly how much stealth was required?

That had been his first mistake. Unbeknown to 18 he'd already made a second, and this one had been even more fatal than the first. By running away he'd missed the arrival of the Duke and the others and now they were inside, beyond the reach of his thermal image finder.

All that 18 saw was Chen, walking the perimeter with a shotgun on his shoulder. And all he could hope for was that Chen did not see him.

CHAPTER 4

Sebastian was lost in his own thoughts, most of which concerned just how fruity Vanessa was likely to be. She was at that age where she'd probably seen and done most things by now. And these power-broking city high-flyers were all into weird stuff; that was well known. At least that was what the lads on his cleaning crew reckoned: bondage, S&M, latex and orgies. And that was at the politer end of the spectrum. They were on a different wavelength to normal people. They needed more extreme thrills to get them going.

Sebastian was no shrinking violet but he knew what he liked and knew what he didn't. Some people might've said, "How do you know until you've tried it?" to which Sebastian would've replied, "I've never smacked my hand with a hammer but I suspect I wouldn't like that either".

One of the guys had told him not to worry about it. If she wanted to try something he wasn't entirely comfortable with, all they had to do was agree a safety word beforehand – like Peaches or Treacle or Portillo or something. Then, instead of waking up the neighbours by shouting "Ahh, stop it! Stop it! I don't like it!" which, in certain scenarios, could be misconstrued as, "I'm a bad boy, don't stop and give it a twist as you jam it in," all he had to do was say "Treacle" and she'd untie him, yank off the crocodile clips and go and wash her hands. It didn't exactly fill Sebastian with confidence but at least he had a plan.

"Who are you?" a voice from out of nowhere said to break his train of thought.

Sebastian jumped out of his skin and almost swung a punch in the opposite direction.

"Jesus! What the fuck are you doing creeping up on people like that? You looking for a smack in the gob or something?" he said to the eight and ten year old lads who were standing just behind him.

"Waiting for someone, are you?" the ten-year-old asked.

"Shows does it?" Sebastian replied.

"You don't live around here, do you?" the boy now observed.

"Thank God for that," said Sebastian, looking out across the car park at the moonlit fields and silent skeletal trees. "What a dump!" Anywhere with this little neon was clearly a shit-hole.

The boys weren't dressed for the countryside. They were more like the street kids Sebastian saw on his Hackney estate with their fake designer brands and pony sportswear and yet here they were, unaccompanied and unconcerned by the stranger in the midst. Perhaps they were meeting Vanessa too?

"Shouldn't you be in bed by now boys?" Sebastian said, pointing to the station clock that had ticked past nine o'clock and was still going strong.

"My bed time's not till ten," the older lad said.

"Ten o'clock! That's outrageous. I was never allowed to stay up till ten when I was your age," Sebastian said, self-consciously inching his way towards middle age with statements like that.

"What a dick!" the younger one quite rightly concluded.

Without further ado, the older one introduced himself and his brother as Mick and Nick, commissars of Christ's Hospital and all it encompassed. Mick further went on to explain how he and Nick were on the lam from their mum for a little family high jinx that had got out of hand.

"Give us a quid," Mick then said, as that seemed to be the way the conversation was drifting.

"What for? For pushing your sister into a pond?" Sebastian asked, recapping the events of the preceding anecdote.

"No, for sweets," Mick clarified.

"Ain't your old man ever told you about talking to strangers?" Sebastian warned them.

"Ain't yours?" little Nick countered.

"Weren't there to tell me nothing. I grew up in an orphanage. Never even knew him," Sebastian explained and a look of shared pain fell upon Mick's face.

"My dad's in Afghanistan," he said quietly, looking away into the middle distance. At that moment Sebastian saw he wore years he'd yet to live on his tiny shoulders.

"Oh, is he?" he said, feeling a little guilty at how he'd tried to give them both the brush off. He reached into his pocket and plucked out a shiny £1 coin to make it up to them. It would bring more happiness in their hands than his anyway. "Here, have this then,"

Mick reached for it and have Sebastian a grateful smile.

"Is he in the army then, your old man?" Sebastian asked.

"No," Mick laughed, "the Taliban."

Sebastian was at once outraged and embarrassed at being mugged off by a ten-year-old. It usually took someone at least five years older than Mick to get the better of him when he had his wits about him.

"Oi, give me my quid back!" Sebastian demanded, but Mick just shock his head and passed it to his smiling brother.

"Sorry mate, no refunds," he said, informing Sebastian of company policy.

But Sebastian wasn't about to leave it there. It wasn't the money, it was the principle; although it was also the money. But mostly the principle. And the money. He might've been small for his age but he was twice the size of Mick and Nick and not averse to mopping the car park with the pair of them for whatever pennies they had on them. He'd had it done to him often enough as a kid and it had done him no harm. Also, what with the Station Master back in his little control booth and distracted by a soggy copy of *Mayfair* he'd found on the tracks, there was no one around to stop him. But Christ's Hospital's finest had timed their scam perfectly. A set of beaming bright headlights swept across the car park just as Sebastian had a hold of Mick's collar and suddenly he had bigger fish to fry.

"Here, have that," Sebastian said, shoving his half-finished can of lager at Mick as a parting gift before grabbing his bag and striding out towards the metallic blue door that had just popped open.

Sebastian chucked his bag on the back seat and attempted a clumsy embrace with Vanessa. They'd not done it yet. In fact they'd not done anything yet and Sebastian still had that faint tingle of doubt scratching away at the back of his mind that she'd actually asked him away this weekend to take him to a Scientology conference.

Vanessa returned Sebastian's embrace with interest, pressing her ruby red lips to his to fill his senses with her sweet essence. She was even more alluring that he remembered, with perfect milky skin and just a few strands of jet-black hair hanging free to mask the twinkle in her piercing blue eyes. She wasn't quite Sebastian's fantasy woman, but he was more than willing to rewrite his fantasies for Vanessa. She was everything and more: confident, beautiful and hungry. She was going to gobble him up tonight. And he couldn't wait.

"You smell lovely," he told her as if she was a plate of pork chops.

"And you smell of booze," Vanessa replied, taking the compliment and running with it.

"What? Oh no," Sebastian said, chiding himself for not remembering to Smint-up before she'd got here. "Just a couple with the lads while I was waiting, like."

Sebastian had meant a couple of beers at London Bridge with two workmates while he'd waited to catch his train but Vanessa glanced passed him at Mick and Nick swapping his half-empty can backwards and forwards and raised a quizzical eyebrow.

"I see," she said, leaving it at that.

"So how far's this place then?" Sebastian asked.

"Not far," Vanessa replied, not wanting to spoil the surprise.

"Is there going to be any grub when we get there because I'm starving?" he asked.

"There might well be," she tantalised.

Mick and Nick watched as Vanessa's Jag pulled away, out of the car park and into the night until all it became was a distant hum on the wind.

"Nice looking motor," Mick observed.

"Nice looking bird," Nick observed further, taking a chug on the all-but-dead can and handing it back to his brother.

Mick drained the last few dregs and nodded in agreement.

"I would," he concurred, giving his considered verdict.

CHAPTER 5

Boniface had barely paused for breath for15 minutes. He knew the only way to get some kind of accord was by making as big a pain-in-the-ass of himself as he could. Luckily, this was not only something he was willing to do, it was also something he was born to do. His mother had told him from a very early age that he had a temperament to offend a sunny day. In some ways she'd been right. In others, she'd been very wrong indeed.

He could still see his mother's face. It was etched into his mind forever. But he didn't see her as other sons saw their mothers, all smiling and laughing and wrinkly and warm. He saw her as a head on a spike, strewn along the bastions of the enemy's camp along with the rest of his family. He had been the only one to escape the axe and had taken refuge in the woods like a coward and a thief. He'd run from a lost battle and had exchanged an honourable death for a shameful life but it had been an astute trade. His needless sacrifice would've been scant compensation to his already-pruned family so he ran, away from the blades, away from the carnage and away from his kin, into the forest to hide.

But Boniface hadn't got away. He'd merely stumbled out of one frying pan and into the fire, for lurking on the fringes of the battle was an even more terrifying foe, one that offered not just death but eternal damnation. Ordinarily Boniface wouldnot have had a prayer against such a beast but the fates took pity on this wretch of a man and had other plans in store for him. For the monster that stalked Boniface was not the normal ferocious and unstoppable fiend of folklore, but a reasonable being who hated death almost as much as he created it.

The Duke only took what was necessary and never killed for sport. His favourite tactic was to follow troops into battle and pick over the mortally wounded as they lay dying on the fringes. In his mind this served three purposes: it spared the living, it allowed him to feed without detection and it was safer than tackling those still swinging swords.

31

He might have claimed more people than the plague but deep down the Duke was still a decent sort of soul, or at least he would've been had he not sold it to the devil a thousand years earlier.

Moreover, he was a pragmatist, so when he snatched Boniface into the shadows and away from human eyes, it wasn't to squeeze him like an orange, but to tether him like an ox.

"Transportation. I go north, into the winter. I need an attendant. My previous squire let me down," the Duke said, which was something of a slur considering his last bloke had been hacked to pieces after wandering too close to the battle looking for horses.

"I will obey," Boniface duly gasped ready to agree to anything to stop this ungodly creature from digging its claws into his throat any deeper. "Please!"

"Call me… Master."

And so that was that, a beautiful friendship was born. The Duke tutored, Boniface served and after a thorough apprenticeship he was given the gift himself. That had been more than two thousand years ago. And while Boniface still respected The Duke, he no longer called him "Master".

"You have your rightful quotas," the Duke barked, finally raising his voice in an effort to silence his former *familiar*.

Thomas rasped his lips in impudence until Boniface shot him a look. Boniface had been the Duke's underling, but Thomas was his and the Coven only worked if each man knew his place.

"It's not enough," Boniface continued.

"Nobody's starving," Henry said. Henry had come to the Coven only five hundred years ago so he was still regarded as the new boy. He'd also arrived courtesy of the Duke, so he and Boniface were like brothers to each other – or at least step-brothers who'd taken an instant disliking to each other. Boniface saw himself as his own man but Henry behaved as if he were still in service. He was a kiss-ass and a puppet and despite being immortal, Boniface had no time for him.

"Sixty million, and we're living off scraps," he said, addressing his point to the Duke as if Henry wasn't even there.

"I can speak with the European Council again but you know what they'll say," the Duke shrugged. This was his tried and tested fallback position. If anyone ever proposed something that he didn't agree with – and wouldn't take no for an answer – he would always tell them he'd have to run it past the kings in the high castle but that he wasn't particularly hopeful. It was a classic tactic and one that had been used by nobles, warriors and blokes down at Kwik Fit since before the dawn of time.

"Fuck the Council! I say we set our own quotas," Boniface snapped. He was getting frustrated and it was starting to show.

"And cut our own throats?" Angel said, now pacing the dusty farmhouse kitchen herself. Angel didn't like sitting and she didn't like being confined. This meeting had barely begun and it was already taking too long.

"The Council would hunt us down and you know it," Henry reminded Boniface.

"These are difficult times – for everyone," the Duke said, touching on a conciliatory note. "The glory days are long gone. We must not dwell on the past, lest we become consigned alongside it.

"You what?" Thomas snorted.

"Embrace the future, as I do," the Duke elaborated. "It's better to be a part of it than not."

This was a matter of opinion. Boniface didn't care for the future. Or indeed the present. Where once they'd roamed like lions, now they scurried like rats. Their prey had got the drop on them. Their only hope had been to disappear, to drop out of man's conscience and into folklore. It had been a tactical manoeuvre but Boniface couldn't help but feel he was running from the fight all over again.

"Difficult times!" he exclaimed. "But only for us because I know what they're taking over in Europe and it's a hell of a lot more than what we are over here."

"We are an island race Peter. We have to tread more carefully. This has its pros, and its cons," the Duke said.

"Huh, what are the pros again?" Thomas snorted once more.

"The population's skyrocketing," Boniface reminded them all.

"And so is their technology," Henry said. "Dental records, computer files, DNA. We're not dealing with Bow Street Runners any more."

Looking around this farmhouse Boniface might've been forgiven for thinking he was still in the 18th century. The fixtures and fittings would've been considered old hat by Jack the Ripper while the less said about the actual state of the place the better. Dust, cobwebs, mould and rot. It didn't so much lend the farm a rustic charm as hold it all together. One ill-advised spring clean and a duster could do more harm to this place than a wrecking ball. Not that there was much danger of that. "Hygiene" was something the Thatchers called to their neighbour, Genevieve, when they saw her out and about.

"Oh come on, all those migrants coming in clinging to the undersides of lorries. No one's going to miss a few of them, surely."

Everyone stopped in surprise and looked around for a moment because for once the author of that sentiment wasn't Boniface. It was sweet white-haired old Alice. She was still knitting away and listening carefully to the conversation and whilst she didn't much care for the dreary Mr Boniface or his methods, she did concede he had a point

"Been reading *The Daily Mail* again, Alice?" Angel concluded.

"All part of the look, my dear," she smiled harmlessly, like a wolf in granny's nightdress.

Before Boniface could expand the point Henry was already popping holes in it. "These migrants aren't as invisible as you might think," he said. "They're harvesting the crops, sweeping the streets, emptying the bins and sending money back to their families so that one day they might join them here in the promised land. They are part of the fabric of this society and they will be missed if we start thinking we can go help ourselves."

"Not by my friends they won't," Alice said, meaning the blue-rinse Brexit brigade she followed around like the grim reaper.

"Wait until your friends are lying on their death beds needing their backsides wiped. See how many of them still want to send Miss Saigon back when she's the one holding the toilet roll," the Duke said.

"I suspect it won't come to that for most of my dear old friends," Alice smiled.

Thomas didn't agree. "I don't like 'em over sixty. Too gamey for my tastes," he said, pulling a face at the thought.

But Boniface was determined to get back on point. "What are we even talking about here? I'm no racist. I'll kill anyone, no matter where they're from, I don't care."

"Oh, that's nice. He's so nice," Henry said.

"And what of their remains Peter?" the Duke asked. "Have you thought about that?"

"I'm only talking about a couple more."

"And a couple more after that?" the Duke said. "And then a couple more. And before you know it the numbers start piling up, the missing are found –"

"– and so are we," Angel said, finishing the Duke's sentence for him to show where her loyalties lay.

Boniface threw up his hands in frustration. "It's not like they're not all out there at each other's throats every Saturday night anyway."

"So is this what you've been doing is it; helping yourself?" the Duke asked.

"Oh yeah, you'd like that wouldn't you? Get a sanction off the Council to get rid of me," Boniface sneered, turning back to his former master and glaring at him through the dirty yellow hue of the room's only ancient light bulb.

The Duke shook his head then dropped his eyes away from Boniface. "I wasn't talking to you Peter."

Boniface was confused. "What?"

Angel echoed the sentiment. "What?"

Eyes flew around the room before finally landing on Thomas. "What? What?" he said.

"Did you really think we wouldn't find out? That the Council wouldn't find out?" the Duke asked.

"What's he talking about?" Boniface demanded.

"I don't know," Thomas said, rising to his feet and backing away towards the door.

"He's been over-feeding," Henry told the room.

"No I haven't," Thomas denied.

"Sixteen over your quota already this year. And the less said about last year the better," the Duke accused.

"That's a lie!" Thomas squawked, but everyone recognised the truth when they heard it.

The Duke sealed Thomas's fate with one final twist of the knot. "And not just over-feeding, he's been taking them young."

Boniface finally twigged. "That lad in the papers?"

"Those lads more like," Henry said, chucking a newspaper on the table for all to see. A couple of young lads smiled up the Coven from the front cover beneath the headline 'OUR HEARTS BREAK'.

"That weren't me," Thomas spluttered. "I didn't do them. Honest, I didn't. I swear it."

But as little as Boniface trusted Henry, he knew he wasn't one to make unfounded accusations.

"You didn't, did you?" he said, turning the full glare of his exasperation away from the Duke and onto Thomas.

Thomas continued to edge around the room, glancing at the various exits and seeing his colleagues now rising from their seats to cover them. This meeting had not gone nearly as well as he'd hoped. He'd always liked meeting up in the past. It was something of a luxury for his kind to be able to drop the pretence and be themselves once in a while. Now suddenly he realised he should've been on his guard all the more.

The looks on his contemporaries' faces told him everything he needed to know. The Duke and Henry were obviously deeply disappointed with him, Angel was aghast, Boniface was shocked and Alice? Her expression rarely betrayed her true feelings, which made her the most dangerous of the lot.

Thomas now felt the confines of the farmhouse. He longed to be on the outside, in the open ground with a healthy head start over those he'd called his friends. All he needed was a few yards. Henry and Angel were quick, but Thomas could be quicker still when the grim was at his back.

"I didn't. I didn't. I... I..." he started to lie before realising he was going to have to change his tactics if he wanted to buy himself some time. He turned on Boniface and tried to muddy the waters with a strategic accusation of his own. "You're always saying we should take who we like."

All he needed was plant enough of a seed of a doubt in the minds of the others to buy himself a second chance then that was it, he was out of here and to hell with the Coven and their rules.

But Boniface wasn't biting and shook his head in despair.

"Not like this. Not without consent."

"He'll get us all sanctioned, the imbecile," Alice finally said, throwing her chips in with the others.

"But you said..." Thomas whimpered before pointing around the room. "And you. And you. And you."

The Coven cocked their collective heads.

"Okay, okay, I'll stop. I'll stick to my quotas from now on. I promise. I won't let you down again," Thomas promised, now appealing directly to the Duke.

"If only it were that simple," the Duke glared.

Thomas's mind was already working on a plan B. The first to come near him would lose their eyes, the next their throats. His claws started to stiffen and his teeth started to swell in anticipation. He'd come into this world kicking and screaming so much that he'd killed his own mother in the process, and he'd make darn sure he didn't go into the next without taking a few of his colleagues for company.

But the arrangements had been made. And the trap had been set.

Chen had returned without Thomas noticing, though this time he didn't set down the shotgun as he entered. Instead he pointed it directly at Thomas's guts...

... and pulled the trigger.

CHAPTER 6

18 heard the shot and instinctively ducked. He could tell from the muffled crack that it had been fired indoors and hadn't been aimed his way but 18 had a simple philosophy: it was better to duck at shots that hadn't been aimed at him than neglect to duck at those that had. This tactic had seen him through three wars and one marriage and he wasn't about to change it anytime soon. Particularly not tonight.

No further shots followed, just screaming and pleading. 18 couldn't make out the words but he recognised the tone. It sounded the same in every language.

As it happened Thomas was speaking English but in his anguish he'd slipped into her native dialect, a version of English not spoken since before the Armada had set sail. "... náwiht... hámsócn... álynian... mildheortnes... liss..."

Henry was of a different time so the words meant nothing to him but like 18 he recognised the vernacular. "Please don't kill me." It didn't make any difference. Thomas's time had come. His sentence had been passed. Now it was time to carry it out.

Angel and Chen had Thomas by the arms. The shot had knocked him into his chair and the Duke's lieutenants kept him pinned him in place, defenceless and begging for mercy – just as Thomas's young victims no doubt had.

Henry looked around for an implement to finish the job but found only iron pokers, horse brasses, egg cartons, some forgotten dusty booze and a smattering of pictures of Granny Thatcher. Not too much to bother Thomas with, so Henry improvised and snapped a leg off of a nearby chair with his inhuman strength.

"This isn't right!" Boniface objected, confronting the Duke in one last attempt to save his underling.

"Maybe not," the Duke conceded, the stress of the decision etched across his face, "but it is official." He pulled a parchment of paper from his pocket and handed it to Boniface. There it was in black & white (and some red), an official sanction of execution from the High Council in Budapest. Nothing could be done for Thomas once it had been signed. All the Coven could do was cut their own throats if they refused to comply. "Do it quick!" the Duke told Henry. "Finish this!"

The chair leg hadn't snapped well. It was practically blunt. But Angel and Chen couldn't hold Thomas there while Henry went off to sharpen it. It would have to do. Thomas would have to suffer the agonies of a blunt death. There were no other choices.

Thomas switched back to modern English for one last plea and appealed directly to his former friend. "Please Henry, don't do it!"

But Henry just gritted his teeth and told him, "Sorry Thomas, you did it to yourself," before plunging the makeshift stake into his chest and through his racing heart.

18 heard the scream from way up on the hill, almost as if it had been hollered into his ear. He'd never heard anything like it in his life. From either man nor beast.

Each soldier in the Synod's private army had been issued with a little silver crucifix instead of dogtags. The guys had thought of them as a joke and refused to wear them except for inspection. 18 now dug his from his tunic pocket and put it on.

This joke was no longer funny.

Once his life force had ceased it didn't take long for Thomas's body to crumble. A grey hue sapped the colour from his face, his hair fluttered to the ground and his clothes fell in on themselves. Within a few short minutes of the stake being plunged no trace of Thomas's unnatural time on earth remained.

Angel swept his vestiges into a bag while the Duke bowed his head and recited the Coven eulogy.

"*His journey done, his race now run, the thread that stitched his life unspun… go quietly into the wind our brother, and may your ashes find absolution.*"

"Amen," echoed Henry somewhat inappropriately as he threw the dusty bundle that had once been his comrade into the Thatchers' filthy cellar without so much as a backwards glance.

Boniface seethed. He'd come here with a purpose only to discover that he'd not been the only one. Once again the Duke had won the day.

He didn't condone what Thomas had done. He'd violated Coven rules. There was no coming back from that. Boniface liked to talk about going it alone but he would've never really done it. Not really. It was just a negotiating position: something to force the Duke and the Council's hand. Why hadn't they let him intercede? He could've spoken to Thomas. Brought him back into the fold.

Well Boniface wasn't about to let this go. As he watched his treacherous cohorts right the furniture and straighten the tablecloth to continue with their pissy little meeting, he swore to himself that he would avenge his friend. It didn't matter if he lived another 3000 years, he would hold them to account for what they had done.

As it turned out, Boniface wouldn't have quite so long to wait.

*

"Your mates a farmer then or something?" Sebastian asked, as their headlights finally reached the end of the bumpy dirt track to illuminate the Thatchers' rusty sign above their rusty gate.

"We're just here for the night," she told him, once more giving nothing away that she didn't have to.

The drive from the station had been much the same. Vanessa hadn't even mentioned they'd be meeting anyone else until they'd turned off the main road and into the wilds. Sebastian wondered if he could find his way back to civilisation if he needed to and concluded he probably couldn't. In fact he wasn't even sure where the main road was any more. Left, right, left, right, down winding narrow tracks and through a bubbling ford. The trees crowded in from all sides to shut out the stars, making the night seem impenetrably black, at least until they reached the farm. Then the track opened up, the fields rolled out before him and the moon glistened from on high to douse the distant gothic farmhouse in an eerie silvery light.

"This ain't nothing kinky is it?" he asked warily.

"Describe kinky," Vanessa replied, less than reassuringly.

"I'm not looking to cross the streams if you know what I mean."

Vanessa didn't. She hadn't grown up in an orphanage with few board games and no telly where one of the few available pastimes was seeing how many boys could piss into the same toilet at once, which invariably ended in extra washing for the orphanage.

"I'm just saying, you know, that I like *you*," Sebastian said, emphasising the "you" in the hope of swaying her into turning around and heading back to this mythical flashy hotel as promised.

"I like you too Sebastian," Vanessa replied, adding, "And I'm sure my friends will too."

"I just thought, when you asked me away for the weekend, that it would be just the two of us, you know?"

"Aren't you just the cutest when you're being shy," Vanessa giggled.

"Slightly patronising, but okay," Sebastian shrugged, scratching his head in absence of anything better to say.

"We won't stay for too long. Just a quick bite and then off to bed. I promise," Vanessa said, for once being entirely honest with Sebastian.

Sebastian felt partially reassured and conceded, "Okay, I can live with that."

Vanessa smiled intriguingly. "We'll see."

Waiting for them as they pulled up in front of the farmhouse was Chen, still wearing his sunglasses but no longer sporting his shotgun. Sebastian felt Chen's eyes on him as he climbed from the car despite not being able to see them. Chen didn't smile but he looked like he might do at any minute. But at what, Sebastian wasn't sure.

"Hey Chen. So wonderful to see you again," Vanessa said, smothering Chen in a warm embrace. Or at least as warm as they could manage between them. "Everybody here?" she asked.

"Everybody *was*," he replied codedly, telling her all she needed to know.

"This is Sebastian," Vanessa said, introducing her old and new friends to each other.

"Hey Sebastian. Glad you could make it," Chen said, giving Sebastian a sense that he knew about him already.

"You took the words right out of my mouth, mate," Sebastian half-heartedly replied.

"You go inside. They're all waiting. I'll take care of this," Chen said, jumping in the driver's seat and valet parking Vanessa's Jag around the back and out of sight of prying eyes.

"Come on," Vanessa said, leading Sebastian up the garden path – literally.

"But he's got my bag!" Sebastian objected. Vanessa disappeared through the front door without waiting for Sebastian. As much as he wanted to go back to the station, go back to London and go back to the pub, he was going nowhere without a lift and his train ticket and he knew it. "Fuck's sake!" he muttered to himself, reluctantly following his date out of the freezer and into the frying pan.

18 had seen the car arrive but not who'd got out. His vantage point was all wrong and view was trained on the rear of the property, as had been his approach through the woods. He contemplated moving but decided against it. He was happy where he was. If Colonel Bingham wanted someone to reconnoitre the front door he could go up and knock on the fucking thing himself. 18 was sitting tight tonight. He'd seen and had enough. It was time to do something different, be a carpet fitter or open a fish & chip shop, and tomorrow that was precisely what he was going to do.

All he had to do was finish tonight's shift and retire with honour.

CHAPTER 7

Sebastian stared around the room he now found himself in. It was just about as far away from the room he'd pictured himself standing in this weekend as it was possible to be. Dilapidated, dirty, dim and dusty, the place would've sent a shiver down Doris Stokes's spine had she not been plying her trade from the other side these days.

Six faces stared up at him, awaiting his verdict. Sebastian gave them all the once over and although he didn't know their names just yet, he sized them up all the same. There was Vanessa – sweet Vanessa – whose face Sebastian had been hoping to get better acquainted with this weekend; Angel, a girl closer to his own age of undefined mixed race but clearly define beauty (would it be impolitic to part-exchange Vanessa for a crack at her tonight?); Henry, a beardy tree-hugger he suspected swung every way possible including a few ways he'd invented just for this evening; the Duke, a headmaster-a-like who looked like he was on the run from one of those Panorama paedo programmes; Alice, a sweet-looking white-haired old lady who looked like she'd sucked more Werther's Originals than he'd had hot dinners; and finally, lurking in the shadows, the ginger whinger to end all ginger whingers, Boniface, a joyless blackhole of doom who glared at Sebastian in open-mouthed consternation as if he'd just walked dog shit into the house and had started tap-dancing across the room.

"Hello everyone, I hope we're not too late," Vanessa said by way of a greeting.

"Not at all. Your timing could not be better," the Duke replied with a smile.

Boniface was still staring at Sebastian. He hadn't blinked in almost thirty seconds and it was making Sebastian's eyes run just trying to keep pace with him.

"I don't fucking believe this," was all he could finally say.

"You know the rules, Peter, one out, one in," the Duke declared, standing an upturned chair back onto its legs as he made his way across to greet their half-expected guest.

"So nice to be consulted," Boniface growled.

"If there's a problem, I can always piss off to the boozer," Sebastian selflessly volunteered. Just say the word, he secretly prayed. He was just about ready to run all the way back to London Bridge.

"Oh no no, not at all, er... ?" the Duke said, suddenly realising he didn't know this young man's name.

Sebastian didn't guess what the Duke's "er" indicated so he just replied with one of his own. "Er...?"

"Your name?" the Duke finally clarified.

"What about it?" Sebastian asked in confusion.

"This is Sebastian," Vanessa introduced before adding ominously. "He's the one I told you about."

"Fine name, Sebastian," was the Duke's considered verdict. Everything about Sebastian was to be judged tonight, even his name, which was something he'd had no control over. That had been left to the Policeman who'd driven him to the orphanage as a baby after he'd been found abandoned in a shopping centre toilet. The Policeman had always longed for a son of his own, so that he could call him after his Olympic hero, Sebastian Coe. As fate would have it, he and his wife were to only have daughters, all of them no doubt called Sally Gunnell.

"Thanks. Always hated it myself," Sebastian frowned, annoyed that despite having loads of Steves he could've chosen from (Steve Ovett, Cram, Redgrave & Backley etc) the copper had still named him fucking Sebastian.

"What do your friends call you then?" the Duke asked in the hope of making him feel more at ease.

Sebastian thought about that one and concluded, "Sebastian".

"Very telling," was Boniface's equally considered verdict.

"I'm the Duke," the Duke said, giving Sebastian a little aristocratic bow.

"You're a duke?" Sebastian replied, not quite understanding if that was his name or title.

"He's *the* Duke," Boniface corrected, directing the little upstart to mind his place.

"Why not? I'm game," Sebastian shrugged, deciding not to question anything again. In and out, that's all he wanted to do. Hello, goodbye, right we're off.

"Don't mind him, he's harmless," Vanessa told Sebastian, which wasn't entirely truth. "He is—"

"Nothing to you!" Boniface snapped, turning away from Sebastian to give him the cold shoulder.

Henry took a different approach and offered Sebastian a smile and his hand. "Hello, I'm Henry. So you're the gypsy boy we've heard so much about?"

Sebastian didn't think of himself as a gypsy. He may have been by blood but his roots were firmly planted in the concrete jungles of Tower Hamlets. What did it matter who his parents were when they'd left him to the world with nothing more than a grubby blanket and a grubby plea for forgiveness scrawled upon the toilet paper all those years ago?

But Sebastian conceded the point, albeit with one small caveat. "Romani," he said.

"I meant no offence," Henry reassured him, then he gave him a little wink. "I hail from the East myself."

Sebastian accepted his hand and almost recoiled at how cold Henry's clasp was. "Cor dear, yeah, Siberia was it?" he said, snatching his hand back only to have it yanked from him once again but Angel and then Alice in quick succession, each of them warding fingers of ice. Sebastian finally got it. This must've been some sort of bad circulation club or ice holding society. There was no other possible explanation.

"Get some gloves you lot," he advised as they drifted back to their seats and retook their places at the table.

"Shall we begin?" the Duke suggested, glancing between Sebastian and the final vacant chair to prompt him to join them.

Sebastian dithered for a moment, wondering what they were about to start and concluding he didn't want to know. Why did they need him? He didn't know anyone here. Couldn't they just get on and play strip poker or whatever it was they had in mind without him? There were already more blokes than birds anyway and he had no desire to see Alice drop her knitting anytime tonight.

"Come," Vanessa urged him, pulling him to the table with her eyes.

Sebastian knew there was no way around it, he had to hear them out, so he took a seat and had barely rested a buttock when the room tumbled sideways and he found himself on the floor looking up.

The underside of the table was even filthier than the rest of the room. Bits of old food and indiscernible nastiness festered down here to give it a slightly repellent subterranean vibe. Sebastian jumped to his feet as quickly as he could and looked around for the cause of his tumble.

"What the fuck! One of the leg's been snapped off," Sebastian said, turning the three-legged chair he'd been invited to take upside down and doing a quick count. The fourth had been buried into the heart of the last person to sit in that chair but it been forgotten in the heat of the moment and Henry reprimanded himself for the oversight.

"Here, have mine," he offered in an effort to make amends.

"No, take mine," Angel echoed, wanting to laugh but knowing she ought not to.

"Oh no, you're alright. Don't worry about it," Sebastian said, tossing his chair aside and wondering his he'd found himself a loophole out of the forthcoming debate.

"Take it Sebastian," Vanessa told him.

"No no seriously, I'll wait in the car," he volunteered, already heading towards the door.

"SIT DOWN!" the Duke commanded before softening his approach with a "please."

Once again, Sebastian took a deep breath and joined these oddballs at the table, having first double-checked his next chair had a full complement of legs in case it turned out this was some sort of running joke.

"We have a proposal for you," the Duke told him solemnly.

"I thought you might," Sebastian said, bracing himself for the worst.

"We are eight in number," the Duke began.

"We have always been eight," Angel said from the other side of the table.

"Since before the times of *Upir*," Alice chipped in.

"The Council decrees it," Henry said.

"Do they?" Sebastian said. "Yeah my council's a bit like that. Drives me mad, bleeding jobsworths hey. Mind if I smoke?" He pulled a cigarette from the packet in his pocket and lit it without waiting for permission. Not only did he need it, he also figured they might asked him to smoke it outside, giving him the perfect opportunity to sit this initiation shit out and slip off to the pub. The Station Master might not have thought there were any boozers around here but Sebastian was confident he could find one with enough of a head start.

"But this night, Sebastian, we are seven," the Duke declared.

"There is a space," Angel said.

"If not a chair, hey? Hey?" Sebastian guffawed, looking around for laughs but finding only stony faces. "Fucking nora!"

"Sebastian, please, this is important. Just listen to what the Duke has to say," Vanessa implored him.

The temperature in the room plunged a couple of degrees despite the filthy black AGA smoking away in the fireplace. Nobody said anything for a moment except the grandfather clock to Sebastian's right. It chimed with a dull brassy clunk to let Sebastian know it was ten o'clock. The night was passing swiftly but this moment seemed to linger on forever.

The Duke found his smile again, although it had lost some of its lustre.

"Vanessa has spoken very highly of you. She says you come from... good stock."

This was news to Sebastian. "You're joking ain't you? I'm a Romani from an orphanage. I'm all back catalogue and no band."

"That'll work for us," Henry told him ominously.

Sebastian wasn't sure which of them to turn away from first. All eyes lingered on him as if he were a particularly succulent cut of sirloin hanging in a butcher's shop window.

47

"Look," Sebastian smiled apologetically, "I'd love to and all that but you know, you caught me on a bad week, I'm all tapped out." He patted his pockets to illustrate the point but assured them: "It's a shame because normally I'm the man to see, yo!"

"The boy's an idiot," Boniface concluded. Sebastian warmed to him in that moment. If he could windBoniface up in such a short space of time then surely it was not beyond his considerable powers to annoy the rest of them enough to earn himself the boot before last orders.

"No honest, I mean, sounds brilliant and all that, whatever it is, save the whale or praise Jesus or whatever it is you've got going," Sebastian said, second-guessing tonight's mystery buzz word. "It's just… you know… I like to do my own thing, plough my own furrow, fly my own flag, so no offence and all that, and seriously thanks for asking but I might just…"

As he spoke, the smoke from his cigarette found its way up Alice's nose and brought about an unstoppable sneeze that momentarily restored her unnatural appearance. She quickly recovered but not before she'd treated Sebastian to her full-on Nosferatu, with blood-red eyes, vicious fangs and cadaverous leathery skin to knock him onto his back him for the second time in as many minutes. "Shit! Fuck! Shit!"

Sebastian scrambled away from Alice and jumped to his feet. No one else moved. No one else seemed to have noticed.

"Did you see that? Did you see her?" Sebastian jabbered, pointing an accusatory finger at Alice, who by this point had regained her composure and resembled a sweet white-haired old lady once again.

The Duke turned to Vanessa. "You didn't tell him?" he said.

"I thought we'd break it to him gently," she shrugged.

"She's a monster! Miss Marple's a fucking monster!"

"Calm down Sebastian. It's quite alright," the Duke reassured him, taking to his feet and approaching slowly to show him he was amongst friends.

"But she's a zombie," Sebastian protested, oblivious to the fact that it wasn't just his Romani heritage that rendered him a minority in this circle.

"Sebastian, it's cool," Henry smiled sympathetically, joining him in the corner of the room, which was where Sebastian's back had finally met the wall.

"But... but... but... but..." Sebastian but-but-butted.

It was then and only then that his eyes now fell upon a dusty mirror on the far side of the kitchen. The room was so gloomy that he'd not noticed it before but now that he did he finally saw the problem.

His was the only reflection staring back at him. His own.

There was no trace of Henry, the Duke, Alice, Angel, Boniface or... even Vanessa. He'd stepped through the looking glass and was now in the land beyond.

The Duke followed his gawking eyes and confirmed: "We're not saving the whale here, Sebastian."

"And we're certainly not peddling God," Henry concurred.

"We are seven," Vanessa said stepping forwards and into Sebastian's line of sight. "And tonight we must become eight."

One by one they all now stood to face Sebastian, blocking what little heat there was coming off the fireplace to send the temperature in the room plummeting further.

"Oh – fuck!" Sebastian shuddered accordingly.

"Oh fuck indeed, my young Romani friend," Henry sympathised with a wry smile. And it was heartfelt indeed. So much to take in. So little time. Henry had been there himself and remembered the moment well. All his closely held beliefs had been blown away in a heartbeat and only his blind acceptance had ensured his survival. Now it was Sebastian's turn. But was it a gift or a curse? That was a philosophical question. And no man could answer for another.

"We have a vote before us," the Duke announced, turning to the others in a way that suggested Sebastian was no longer part of the discussion, merely the object of it. "Yay or nay. Let us hear it now."

Vanessa was the first to raise her hand. "Yay," she said automatically. It would've been pretty odd and a big waste of everyone's weekend if she'd vetoed her own candidate.

"Yay," Angel echoed.

"Yay," Alice smiled sweetly.

"Yay," agreed Henry. "And Chen's a yay as well," he said, casting their sentry's vote by proxy.

The Duke was just about to rubberstamp the decision with a "Yay" of his own when Boniface dropped a dirty great filthy bluebottle into everyone's ointment with a resentful sniping "Nay."

"Nay?" the Duke snapped.

"Aye, nay," Boniface confirmed. "Next time you want to change the faces around here perhaps you'll ask me first."

"Nay? What's nay mean?" Sebastian asked warily, keeping his fingers cross that it meant he could go home now.

"Just for spite? Just petulance?" the Duke raged, incensed at his former charge's malevolence.

"Thomas was my underling. I brought him in. You should've talked to me first!" Boniface snarled, meeting the Duke's glare of disgust without showing so much as a flicker of shame.

Sebastian sought a clarification.

"Nay? What's nay mean?"

Vanessa now turned on Boniface and shouted: "I spent months on his candidature. He's twelve generations pure. You can't do this."

"Can't?" Boniface said, his snarl now turning to a strangled smile in a gloom of the shadows. "I can and I am. And there's nothing you can do about it, not without another sanction. And I take it you didn't bring two of them with you tonight, huh?"

The Duke watched as Boniface scrunched up Thomas's sanction, lifted the stove's charred lid and dropped it into the flames.

"Subtitles anyone?" Sebastian requested.

The Duke pursed his lips and let out a resigned sigh. "Our apologies Sebastian," he said, turning and walking away. He

50

could've put Sebastian out of his misery quickly and (relatively) painlessly but he didn't like to kill in front of others. They all fed, of course they had to, but as their leader it didn't feel dignified to do so in public, any more than it would've been for the Queen to deliver her annualtelevised address whilst tucking into aplate of Christmas dinner.

Vanessa now moved in and showed Sebastian her best impression of a frowny face. She felt something for him, she truly did, but not enough to stop her from killing him. He was, after all, only human, and humans were there to serve but two purposes – to feed the Coven and reinforce its numbers when necessary. Boniface's "Nay" had limited Sebastian's options. Vanessa was about to limit them further.

"It wasn't meant to be like this Sebastian," she told him with regret. "I thought they'd all accept you. I didn't count on the fact that some people are just assholes no matter how long they live for."

Boniface let out a sarcastic "Ha!" and got ready to enjoy the show. Unlike some of them present he actually liked the process of killing. Not necessarily in a sadistic way, but Boniface felt it was a privileged responsibility to see a person from this world and into the next. It brought him a closeness he had never known in life and made him feel like an apostle of kinds, albeit one who rode into town accompanied by a plague.

Sebastian now performed the same jig that Thomas had danced earlier, edging himself around the room and in the direction of the door. It wouldn't take a shotgun to stop him in his tracks and Vanessa allowed him to say a few final words. It only seemed right.

"Wait wait wait wait! Six to one, it's a landslide surely?" Sebastian pointed out, stepping on something soft as he slid along the wall and looking down to see it was a stuffed cat.

Vanessa just smiled. "I did like you, Sebastian," she said, as if this would somehow atone for what was about to come.

Sebastian saw an angle and ran with it. "And I liked you too… Vanessa," he said, thanking Christ he remembered her name. He didn't always. "All of you in fact. What good lads." He now turned to Boniface and addressed him directly, as he was obviously the one he needed to win over. "Even you mate. You look alright, all things considered. Go on, take a day to get to know me, we could be mates."

"You're not my type," Boniface glowered, breaking one of his own cardinal rules and conversing with the livestock, although his words were intended for more than Sebastian's ears.

The Duke had seen and heard enough. There was no dignity in this, neither for Sebastian nor the Coven. The decision had been made. Vanessa now had to get on with it. "You brought him here. He's your responsibility," he reminded her. This was true. Protocol dictated the nominee was under the care of the nominator. If Sebastian had been accepted, it would've been up to Vanessa to turn and teach him. As it was, she now had to end things for him. As a veracious feeder, normally this wouldn't have been a problem for Vanessa but this was a normal situation. She didn't normally spend three months getting to know her food before dispatching it.

Sebastian made a dash for a front door but he didn't get to within ten feet of it. Vanessa grabbed him by the arm and forced him to his knees. His death would be quick and clean. It was only right.

"Close your eyes, Sebastian. Think happy thoughts," she advised.

"Oh God no, wait, please, you can't, I've got kids!" he said, lunging at a few final straws in an effort to prolong his [admittedly] shitty life a few more shitty moments.

"No you haven't," Vanessa said. "You haven't got anyone."

It was a lie and it had been quickly rumbled but it had still bought him a few seconds. "I know," Sebastian came clean with a shrug. "I just said that."

From his new vantage point Sebastian spotted a couple of pokers a short tumble away. Before Vanessa could strike the killer blow he launched himself like Jason Statham at the fireplace only to land like Mr Bean. Once he'd untangled himself from the shovel and coal bucket he jumped to his feet and held out two pokers in the form of a crucifix.

"Get back all of you! Get back!" he shouted, finding his inner Van Helsing. "In the name of God, the son and the holy smoke, I command thee to get back!"

Henry wondered if he'd heard right and double-checked with Angel. "Did he just say *thee*?"

Vanessa faltered. Sebastian was determined to make this as hard as possible wasn't he? Some people did that, fought until the bitter end and went out kicking and screaming, often (and curiously) those with the least to live for. It was such a waste. He would've made a fine nightwalker but it wasn't to be.

"I'm sorry Sebastian, I'm afraid it doesn't quite work like that," she told him. Hollywood had much to answer for.

But Sebastian wasn't done there and went straight to Plan B. "No? Well how about this then?"

He swung one of the pokers as hard as he could, catching Vanessa clean across the temple. If she'd been human he would've undoubtedly killed her but Vanessa merely soaked up the blow and stepped back to catch her balance. It was enough to give Sebastian a glimpse of the stairs behind her and he took it, dashing through all six of them and scrambling up to the bedrooms to look for... something... anything...

He didn't know what. Sebastian was now living on a second-by-second basis.

No one moved for a moment. No one went after him. They didn't have to. He wouldn't get far.

Henry traced his finger along the gash in Vanessa's head. It was already heeling and would be gone in another minute.

"It's true what they say, love hurts," he smirked.

Vanessa laughed but the Duke and his former squire looked far from amused at this debacle.

CHAPTER 8

18 was listening intently. No shots had been fired but he could tell something was going off inside the farmhouse. Even from this distance and through solid walls of brick he could hear crashing, smashing and screams of terror – and at one point he even thought he made out the words "fuck off you cunts!" – but he had no idea who or what was behind them.

He checked his watch. An hour had passed since he'd last radioed in. Where the hell was his back-up.

"Right behind you," said a voice as though it had read 18's mind.

18 spun around and reached for his holster. Colonel Bingham was knelt just behind him, barely four feet away. How the hell had he got the drop on him? Jesus, 18 concluded, he wasn't cut out for this anymore. A day comes in every soldier's life when he can no longer cut the mustard and 18's had dropped on him from on high. This had been such a cushy assignment, such a joke of a job, that he'd allowed himself to get sloppy and start thinking about the future. It had taken his edge and if he wasn't careful it would take his life as well.

"Glad to see you're still here, 18," Colonel Bingham said. "What's happening in there?"

"I don't know, sir: yelling, screaming, shouting, all sorts. It's horrible," he told him, still trying to catch his breath.

"And that's your report, is it?" Colonel Bingham said, raising an eyebrow.

"Who else is here, sir? Where's our back-up?" 18 asked.

"Don't worry," Colonel Bingham replied. "We've got it all in hand."

All at once the treeline stirred as the rest of the unit moved into position. Night scopes and infrared cameras were trained on the farmhouse in the valley below. Another Squad crawled through the trees to set up shop on the other side of the farm with a third sitting in reserve with the trucks at the rear.

Just how many men did have Colonel Bingham have under his command tonight?

"All of them," the Colonel said, answering 18's unasked question. "Manoeuvres are over. This is the real thing."

*

Sebastian put his shoulder to the creaking bedroom door. It wouldn't keep them out forever. All it could do was buy him a few seconds. But for what?

He looked around for ideas.

He was in a child's bedroom but it was the sort of bedroom that would give any child nightmares for life. A filthy rocking horse slowly jigged backwards and forwards in the corner, next to an empty cot and beneath the gaze of legion of dust-covered dolls that may or may not have been collected from the scenes of air crashes. Sebastian might have had a deprived childhood but at least he hadn't had this one.

Another crash and another crack appeared in the door. He'd locked it and shoved a chair under the handle but it wouldn't hold. He had to get away and fast.

Unfortunately there was only one way out. And it was a long way down now that he was upstairs.

"Little pig, little pig, let me in," he heard Angel whispering on the other side of the door. CRACK!

A three-foot fissure opened up in the woodwork and the door jam began to splinter. If he stayed where he was they would simply swat him aside when they forced open the door. But it he let stepped away the door wouldn't hold for more than a few seconds. He had no choice. By the hair on his chinny chin chin he had to go for it.

Taking a deep breath he pushed himself off the door and ran full pelt at the window. He dived at it at the last moment, tucking his arms and legs in as he went and braced himself to drop into the cold hard night. But like Sebastian, that Thatchers' knackered old window was tougher than it looked and it bounced him back and dumped him on his arse for a second time tonight.

"What the fuck!" Sebastian swore but the window didn't have time to answer. Another splintering crack from behind him remind Sebastian that time was of the essence, so he scrambled

55

to his feet, hurried to the window again and this time took a moment to unlatch it.

The window swung open easily. And the ground below now beckoned.

A low flat roof led down to an easier drop and Sebastian scurried across it and jumped to the grass, which turned out to be about three foot further down than it looked.

"Oh... my arse!" Sebastian groaned when his legs crumpled beneath him and his fags took the full impact of his descent.

He looked back as he started running. No one had followed him out of the window. Was he in the clear? All he needed was a good head start and he was confident he could lose a bat in this darkness. All he had to do was get to those trees and keep going as far and as fast as he could. Nothing and no one was going stop this particularly Romani, not now he had the ground at his feet and the wind at his back.

... except perhaps the 40 strong detachment of special forces infantrymen who were watching Sebastian running straight for them through infrared crosshairs.

"Get ready," Colonel Bingham said, sliding the safety catch from his SMG from black to red. "On my command..."

18 remembered just in time to review the target through his thermal image detector and found Sebastian easily as a large red blob in the centre of the screen.

"Wait, sir, hot body! He's not our target," he told Colonel Bingham.

Another set of eyes watched Sebastian as he sprinted through the darkness although these did so without the aid of modern military equipment. They were more than capable of peering through the curtain of night as though it were a bright and sunny afternoon.

"He's got spirit. You've got to give him that," Vanessa told Henry as they stood at the kitchen window and watch Sebastian fleeing for his life.

"Yes," Henry agreed. "But he won't get far."

Everyone who was watching thought the same. Only Sebastian was convinced otherwise. And it would be this bloody-minded attitude that would see him through many of the horrors that were to come tonight better than all the firepower currently trained on him put together.

CLUNK!

Sebastian ran headfirst into something immovable. He didn't see where it came from and didn't have time to check his stride. He simply ran straight into it and ended up flat on his back.

Chen looked down at Sebastian and asked, "Going somewhere?"

The guys in the trees hadn't seen him either. He was wearing mostly black so he was hidden against the night but he hadn't registered on their infrared scopes either. He was, for want of a better word, invisible to their technology.

Only now, aided by Sebastian's tumble, did Colonel Bingham actually see him.

"Jesus, where did he come from?"

18 was frantically fiddling with him heat detector and convinced it must be broken because he could still see only one red blob out there, that of Sebastian on the floor currently attempting to scramble across the grass and away from Chen.

"Cold body, sir! Cold body. It's him. It's our target!" he confirmed.

This nugget of intel was overheard half a mile away on a dark and gloomy dirt track by a dark and gloomy man who went by the name of Larousse. He wore a military uniform and military insignia but he was not a military man himself. He also wore a cross and carried a bible but he was not a preacher either. Nobody knew his first name or believed Larousse was really his last. In fact, nobody really knew anything about him except that he paid the bills. And he paid them very very well.

To Colonel Bingham and his men Larousse was an enigma, but to himself he was a modern day crusader, one of the chosen few (otherwise known as the Synod), ready to use his power and wealth to fight the good fight and purge mankind of an evil that had stalked it since Adam and Eve had been ejected from Eden.

Of course, up until now, it had all been largely theory. In the ten years the Synod had been operating in the UK, the luckless Larousse had never once managed to track down a single genuine target. Others on the Continent and further afield had been more successful but Larousse was still on a duck – and a very expensive duck at that.

But now, finally, with all of his forces in the field and the element of surprise still on his side, he finally had one. He had fulfilled his vow. Now all he had to do was make the kill.

It was enough to make his voice tremble as he radioed Colonel Bingham at the front.

"Is it him?" he said, momentarily forgetting to release the speak button. "Colonel Bingham? Colonel Bingham? Do you have a visual confirmation of our target?"

Bingham keyed the handset twice, as was standard procedure when a target was too close to talk but in his excitement Larousse had forgotten the code and kept barking at the Colonel to reply.

Chen strolled after Sebastian, just about far enough for Colonel Bingham to risk a communiqué, so he whispered into his radio: "Confirmed Mr Larousse. We have a positive sighting. The target is cold."

The Colonel's message was barely audible. It sounded more like a shock of static than an actual sentence but Larousse did make out the three key words *"target is cold"*.

Larousse clasped his hands together and gave thanks for being entrusted with such a sacred task. "I am, as always, your obedient servant," Larousse muttered, crossing himself and catching several soldiers nudging one another in amusement.

They would see, he told himself. They would soon bow before the Almighty and recognise His authority on Earth, through the vessel of His apostle.

His divinity secured, all that was left was to give the order so he keyed the handset and told Colonel Bingham to go. "I am giving you the order, Colonel Bingham. Take the target down. On my authority, and that of the Full General Synod, go go go!"

Half a mile away Colonel Bingham rolled his eyes. Someone had been watching too much Ross Kemp. But there it was loud and clear, he had his orders.

"Roger that. Snatch team, on my mark, get ready," Colonel Bingham whispered into his radio, relaying the orders to his men.

All around the treeline safeties were flicked to red and snare poled extended. The target was quick – very quick in fact – but the Unit's bullets were quicker still.

"On my mark!"

Sebastian was still scrambling across the muddy grass with Chen strolling along behind him. Bingham couldn't believe his luck. Their timing was perfect. They would make the kill when the predator was distracted making his own. This would give them best chance of a clean take with only a civilian's death to mess up their paperwork. But he would be simply listed as collateral damage. The Colonel could live with that.

"Get away from me!" Sebastian was screaming. "I mean it. I don't want to fuck you up but I will."

Chen laughed, as did several of the guys in the trees. It was tragic the things people said when the end was nigh. Chen made a grab for Sebastian but Sebastian sprang to his feet and made one last desperate dash for freedom.

"This is it," Colonel Bingham whispered into his radio. "On my count, three... two... "

But Chen didn't run after Sebastian. There was no need. Another arm appeared from out of nowhere and clattered him to the ground once more, this time knocking him out cold.

"Enough arsing about," Boniface scowled. He had other places to be and was not in the mood for this cat and mouse shit.

18 was the first to see him and instinctively grabbed the Colonel's arm to pull him back. "Wait sir, cold body! Second target!"

The Colonel felt his own temperature plunge a couple of degrees and grabbed the thermal imager to check for himself. Sure enough, there it was in red and black, Sebastian lying prone on the floor while two cold figures stood over him.

"Abort the grab! I repeat, abort the grab! Everyone stand down," Colonel Bingham told his men over the airwaves.

Back at the rear, Larousse heard the order without having heard anything else and tried to countermand the Colonel.

"I said go! Take him down. Do it now!" he ordered, terrified that his date with destiny was slipping from his grasp with every passing second.

Colonel Bingham ignored Larousse's demands and knew that his men would too. They answered to him, first and foremost. Larousse might've paid the bills but it was Colonel Bingham who kept his men alive to run them up.

"Colonel! Colonel Bingham. Have you gone yet?" a little tinny voice in Bingham's ear was demanding. "Speak to me!"

But Bingham was about to speak to anyone. Or move. Or even breathe. Because the second target was suddenly looking their way.

"What is it?" asked Chen, looking at where Boniface was looking but seeing only trees. "Peter, what is it?"

"There's something out there," Boniface replied. He hadn't seen anything and he hadn't heard anything, but there was something out there all the same. He could sense it.

Someone else could sense it too and he felt Boniface's eyes burning right into him. He made a dash for it, out of a dip and into the trees with the fear of Satan chasing after him.

"It's just a fox," Chen smiled, "out for his dinner, same as us."

Boniface and Chen turned and walked back to the farmhouse, dragging the unconscious Sebastian with them as they went.

Colonel Bingham now breathed again. How close had they just come to disaster? One target in open ground would've been a challenge. But two targets in open ground – particularly when they'd only planned for one – would've been a quick way to an early grave.

"Let them get back to the house then we move in," he told his men. "Second Squad move up in support."

CHAPTER 9

Boniface dumped Sebastian in a chair and stepped back to jangle his change (his own, not Sebastian's).

"He's all yours," he told them. He was happy to grab Sebastian off the hill but he wasn't about to do the Duke's dirty work for him – particularly not in this suit. It wasn't just the expense but the inconvenience. There weren't many tailors who were prepared to see their clients after dark and Boniface found midday fittings decidedly inconvenient.

The Duke looked at Sebastian. He was as good as dead already but he felt a pang of courtesy all the same.

"Rouse him. It's only proper."

Angel picked the flowers from a nearby vase and tipped the contents onto Sebastian's head. "Wakey wakey, time to die."

Sebastian coughed and spluttered and looked up to see seven horribly familiar faces smiling down at him once again.

"Alright lads, how's it going?" was all he could think to say.

The Duke glanced at Vanessa but Vanessa hesitated, still reluctant to do the necessary. Angel has no such compunctions and grabbed Sebastian's head to give it a spin.

"Alright mate!" she chuckled in response.

"No wait wait wait wait!" he screeched, his voice hitting octaves no man should be able to hit while still in the possession of testicles.

"Just a thought, but do we have any food in tonight?" Vanessa said. "Sebastian was asking earlier."

Vanessa wasn't entirely sure where she was going with this idea but it bought Sebastian a few more seconds nevertheless. Not that he was particularly grateful about it.

"Oh this just gets better and better don't it!" he complained.

To which Angel could only agree. "It would be a shame to waste a meal."

*

A similarly dramatic conversation was taking place in the trees beyond the farm. Colonel Bingham had got on with the job of redeploying his forces without consulting Larousse. There simply wasn't time but Colonel Bingham was a seasoned campaigner and a specialist at reacting to fluid situations. In the armies he'd previously served (not all of whom flew flags you might recognise) he'd been used to using his own judgement to get the job done. All his benefactors had ever asked for were results and plausible deniability. The rest they were happy to leave to God and the ever-reliable Colonel Bingham.

His rank was one of pure fiction. He'd awarded it to himself seven years earlier after killing a Colonel in French Guiana. That had been a good job, lucrative and successful, and it had been the making of him in the private security sector. He'd returned to Europe with his reputation enhanced and a new rank and beret to match (the latter of which required dry cleaning).

But Bingham found that Larousse wasn't like his past patrons. Larousse wanted to be there, on hand and at the kill. He thought his money bought him superiority but all it really bought him was the Colonel's indulgence. This was no way to run an operation.

"Colonel, I demand to know what's going on? I gave you the order to go so why haven't you gone?" Larousse asked over and over again until the Colonel finally answered him.

"There's a second target, Mr Larousse. It changes everything, over."

Larousse's heart skipped a beat at the news. They'd looked for one. They'd found two. It was a miracle. No, divine intervention. Larousse imagined the Synod's reaction when he told them the news in the morning and sent them the ashes of both.

"Understood," he told Colonel Bingham through the radio. "But it changes nothing. We have the resources for two so I'm ordering you to go. Over."

"Father, this is a dangerous situation," Bingham said, deliberately calling Larousse Father because he knew it got under his skin. "We need time to recce the house properly."

"We don't have the time, Colonel," Larousse said, now even more desperate to get the job done before his bats flew their perch. "If the targets are in the house you need to take them down and now."

"But Mr Larousse…" Colonel Bingham started saying only to be cut off by a buzz that indicated Larousse was pressing his talk button at the same time.

"Now Colonel! This is what I'm paying you for!"

*

The vote was a slamdunk. Seven for and only one against.

"Then it's decided," the Duke confirmed.

Sebastian put down his hand.

Angel yanked him back up to his feet with super-human strength and bared her fangs.

"No wait, you can't eat me. I'm all fat and cholesterol," Sebastian pleaded.

"And I've been so good all week," Angel laughed, licking his neck and liking what she tasted. She couldn't stand it when guys over-showered.

She was about to sink her teeth in when the front and back doors burst open and a dozen assault rifles gatecrashed the party. They completely surprised the Coven but not nearly as much as the Coven surprised them.

The soldiers sized up the eight targets before them. Who did they shoot first? Which posed the most danger? How did they grab them all when they'd only brought four snare poles?

Corporal Fenn, who'd been the first through the door, demonstrated a flare for understatements when he keyed his radio to say; "Colonel, we have a problem."

Somewhere to his right, and with his hand hovering over the light switch, Henry could only agree.

"Oh Corporal, you have no idea."

And then, with the merest flick of the switch, the room was plunged into darkness.

CHAPTER 10

Bingham watched on helplessly as the black farmhouse suddenly held an impromptu rave, with blinding strobe lights and a machinegun beat blasting out of every window.

"First Squad come in. 6 are you there?" Bingham was saying into his radio but 6 was already in as many pieces and looking down at his own legs from the chandelier above.

The gunfire lasted only five seconds or so and petered out as each weapon was snuffed. There was a final flurry of movement in the doorway as someone attempted to flee but he didn't make it past the threshold and was dragged back inside with a short-lived scream and the slamming of the door.

Then, as if nothing had even happened, the farmhouse lay still and quiet once more but no one believed it now. The place had shown its hand. Death lurked inside.

18 was breathing hard, almost as if he had sprinted up the hill and away from the fight himself but no one was coming back from there.

Finally the silence was broken by a tinny voice in Colonel Bingham's ear.

"Colonel, how many were in there? Over," Larousse asked.

"More than two, Mr Larousse. More than two," he confirmed. "First Squad over and out."

Everyone heard the communiqué. And everyone knew where the order had originated. Larousse was on borrowed time. Then again, from this moment onwards, they all were.

"There are more of them outside," Henry whispered to the others, holding one of the soldier's earpieces to his own ear as he eavesdroppedin on their inquest.

Boniface crouched by the front window and looked up the slope and towards the line of trees. He should've trusted his instincts and investigated properly. He knew it hadn't just been a fox out there he'd sensed. Bloody Chen. How had he let so many guns creep up on them?

"How many are there?" he asked.

Henry listened for a little longer but shook his head. "I don't know. But they seem to be having the same conversation."

"Okay, Colonel Bingham, tell Second Squad to move into position. You have my authority to go," Larousse told the Colonel, turning his pencil around to rub the names of First Squad out on the map before him.

"Negative Mr Larousse. We're standing fast. The situation has changed and we need time to reassess," Colonel Bingham replied, directing the troops around him to spread along the ridge and plug the gaps left by First Squad.

"Captain Bingham, you may have the experience but I have the authority," Larousse almost shouted, starting to lose patience having to give the same command again and again. "Now I am ordering you to take down our target. Right now. This instant!"

Bingham heard the radio crack between his fingers and eased up his grip a little. Tonight was going to be either a very long one or a very short one for all concerned. One way or another.

"Mr Larousse," Colonel Bingham replied in his most measured tone to disguise the anger that was brewing up inside him, "you have just given out that order over a compromised radio channel. Now before you go sacrificing any more of my men – scramble to pre six. Over."

Larousse went white when he realised his error. He felt someone's eyes burning into him and turned to see the commlink operator turning away in contempt.

They blame me, he suddenly realised. But he wasn't the enemy here. It was those creatures in the farmhouse. They were the ones who'd killed their comrades. They were the enemies of all creation. He was merely a soldier of God, sent here to fight the good fight –

– half a mile from the front.

*

"That's all folks, they've just scrambled," Henry told the other, dropping the earpiece he'd borrowed back into the sticky goo he'd plucked it from.

"Who are they?" Vanessa asked, frisking one of the dead soldiers for ID but finding only ammunition.

"I don't know. But I've got a horrible feeling they know who we are," Henry said.

The Coven were strong, collectively and individually, stronger than the strongest of men, with none – or at least few – of their mortal weaknesses, but their greatest weapon remained their anonymity. What was it that Charles Baudelaire had once said: "the greatest trick the devil ever pulled was to convince the world he did not exist"? Or perhaps that was Kevin Spacey. Either way it was an astute line and one worthy of repeating.

"They're here for us," Henry concluded. "Only something went wrong." He looked around at the snatch Squad and realised, "They didn't expect all of us tonight, maybe just one or two."

With this conclusion came the realisation that they still had the advantage. How much of an advantage he didn't know, but he was fairly sure the entire British Army wasn't waiting for them outside so that gave them a fighting chance.

Chen's nose twitched. "Something's moving."

"It's Sebastian. He's trying to sneak away without saying goodbye," Angel said, pulling the table cloth off Sebastian as he inched his way along the floor and towards the door.

Sebastian's face fell when he realised he'd been rumbled. It had been a good plan. Not perfect but pretty good all things considered. Slither out on his belly under cover of lace and make a break for it while Vanessa and her mates were filling their faces on Brave Two Zero. Given the chance he would've probably tried it again but Henry's steely grip on his ankle told him it hadn't worked this time.

"I wouldn't go out there if I were you, old bean," Henry advised, dragging Sebastian back across the floor and into the bosom of the Coven once more.

*

Colonel Bingham was rearranging his chess pieces in light of the first battle of Thatchers' Farm. He hoped to avoid a second, or at least ensure that it lasted a little longer than the first battle and produced a more positive result for his side. "Second Squad, spread along the southern ridge and hold that line. Third Squad, move up to the outer barns and hold those positions. Four and five take the southern slopes and find cover. I want eyes on every window."

Larousse's voice came hard on the heels of Colonel Bingham's and attempted to countermand his orders.

"No Third Squad, you'll provide support for Second Squad when they move in to take down the targets."

Colonel Bingham could scarcely believe his ears. The definition of insanity, according to Albert Einstein, was to do the same thing over and over again and expect different results. That theory had been tested to its limits in the trenches of the First World War and if Larousse had his way it would be retested tonight. But Colonel Bingham would be damned if he was going to let the underfed donkey on the other end of the line throw his lions to the slaughter.

"There's not going to be any more assaults, Mr Larousse. We're sealing off the perimeter," the mercenary told his patron.

"That's not the plan, Colonel Bingham," Larousse replied, only too aware of how the targets were taken down. He'd attended every training exercise and every live firing drill. He'd seen the footage of successful kills abroad and had read the training manuals. Give him a gun and he could do it himself – if his job wasn't to stay back and oversee the mission as a whole.

"The plan changes when I lose a whole Squad in under a minute. Now we have three Squads left and I'm not throwing away any more of my men for nothing, do you understand?" Colonel Bingham argued.

Larousse couldn't understand the logic of Colonel Bingham's argument. What were the lives of a few soldiers when they stood on the brink of eternal glory?

"Colonel, this is the opportunity of a lifetime. We can't just let them get away," Larousse now resorted to pleading.

"And we won't. We're going to put a ring of steel around this farmhouse until daylight. Nothing gets in or out of there alive tonight. Then tomorrow, we can take that place apart brick by brick until there's nowhere left for them to hide from the sun."

That struck a chord with Larousse. Containment then total extermination with a minimal loss of life, as that seemed to be important to Colonel Bingham for some reason. It seemed like the perfect plan. Perhaps the Colonel did know what he was doing after all? And as Larousse had recruited him, this would surely reflect well on him with the Synod.

Larousse was convinced and sanctioned the change in tactics with a declaration of approval.

"Very good Colonel, carry on."

Half a mile away, Bingham hung up the radio and turned to 18 to share the joyous news. "He says we can carry on," he said, shaking his head

*

The Coven had also been anticipating the next assault and sat like coiled springs ready to pounce the moment the first person to set foot through their door. That no one did, came as something of a genuine surprise to Vanessa.

"They're not attacking," she pointed out, in case no one else had noticed.

"Would you?" Boniface asked, looking around the smoking carnage they were crouched in. Spent cartridges sizzled in pools of blood and dust danced with smoke in front of the building's newest holes to give the place a Stalingrad-like ambiance. Boniface had been there on his holiday at the time so he knew.

"What are we going to do?" Angel asked, looking to the others for suggestions. Angel was a fearsome lone wolf but this was not the time to go off on a solo spree. The enemy outside was like none they had seen before. They were organised, well equipped and knowledgeable. This was no rogue Van Helsing on a mission. This was an extermination Squad. And they'd only just begun.

If the Coven were to see the sun set again tomorrow evening they would have to pool their resources to get the hell out of this mess.

"One thing's clear, we can't stay here all night," Henry said, before noticing one voice had been conspicuous by its absence. "Duke? Duke, what's the plan?"

He looked around for a response but the Duke was nowhere to be seen. The room had been practically demolished in the fight, with bullets, stun grenades and flying body parts littering the place with debris. Henry took a quick roll call and found Alice, Angel, Boniface, Chen, Vanessa and Sebastian all present and correct but no Duke.

Had the enemy got him? Had he fled the scene during the fight?

Angel overturned the upset table and found the Duke beneath. His face was grey and his eyes glassy. The reason was obvious to all. A large splinter of wood, blown off the grandfather clock, had lodged itself into the Duke's chest right where mortal men kept their hearts.

"Oh no no no!" Henry panicked, pulling at the splinter but dislodging only a torrent of black blood.

The Duke winced and turned his eyes towards them. He tried to mouth something but the words were lost on his dying choke.

"Come back to us. Duke, don't go!"

But the decision was not his to make and with one last agonised gasp he slipped beneath the veil of death to crumble to dust in Henry's hands.

"He's gone," Henry said, scarcely able to comprehend this world without the Duke. How would they continue? How would they cope?

Everyone felt the same and their silence betrayed their fears. He'd been the rock of their movement, the closest thing most of them had known to a father and now he was gone. And nothing would ever be the same again.

Boniface had a thought. "Who gets his territory?"

The rest of the Coven glared at him with a mixture of horror and incredulity etched across their faces. Boniface read between the lines and gave a shrug.

"Too soon?"

But this would not be the end of the matter as far as he was concerned. London was now up for grabs. And opportunities like this didn't come around every century.

CHAPTER 11

18 was an astute soldier. He'd learned his trade in various theatres of warfare and now applied this hard won experience to the operation at hand.

"Shouldn't we just get out of here? If they're as dangerous as Larousse says, shouldn't we just jump in the trucks and fuck off as far away as possible?" he suggested.

It was a considered question so Colonel Bingham thought it earned a considered answer. "We've caught the tiger by the tail, 18. As long as we don't let go we won't end up like First Squad. Lights!"

A series of powerful spotlights clunked on all along the ridge to turn night into day. Six of them in picked out the farmhouse below and the surrounding barns to bathe them in a blanket of light from which a spider would've had trouble hiding.

"If anything so much as moves down there, shoot it," Colonel Bingham ordered his troops.

"What if it's one of First Squad?" 18 asked.

"Especially if it's any of First Squad," Colonel Bingham replied without needing to spell out why.

But Bingham needn't have worried. Most of First Squad – or at least what was left of them – had been dumped in the cellar to get them out of the way. It was one thing killing people, it was quite another to have them look at you for the next six hours.

"What about the Duke? Should we get a broom or something?" Vanessa asked, looking down at the pile of ashthat lay before her.

"I saw a dust pan and brush in the cupboard," Alice said, intending the comment to be genuinely helpful.

"Dear God, and who says there's no dignity in death?" Boniface chuckled. "Why don't you just vacuum the poor bastard up and be done with it?"

"Leave him where he is," Henry said. "His problems are over. Ours are just beginning." And with that they uttered the Coven prayer to send the Duke on his way, with each wondering who would be left to recite these same words over their remains when the time came.

Henry squinted through the window and up the hill at the huge lights that blazed back. The light itself couldn't harm them. It was the wrong sort of light. Artificial. Cold. Weak. But it dazzled Henry to the point of blindness. He wasn't used to it. He didn't like it. And it unnerved him. He felt naked without a cloak of darkness in which to operate. He was a mole out of his hole. And the jackals were on the prowl.

"Let's just Skype from now on, yeah?" he suggested.

"What's Skype?" Angel asked.

"You know, that internet phone thingy?" Henry told her, using all the latest technical jargon to prove he understood what he was talking about.

"I can work the video now," Alice said with pride. It had taken her thirty years but she'd finally got the hang of it.

"Are you still using tapes?" Vanessa asked with a smirk.

"Yes? Why? Aren't you?" Alice replied uneasily.

A voice piped up in the darkness. "Jesus, it's like being round me nan's house!" Sebastian said, despite having no nan of his own, just a collective foster carer who played the same role to Sebastian and 250 other kids.

"Oh yeah, thanks for reminding me," Boniface said. "Does someone want to kill the little ratboy now?"

Angel grabbed Sebastian by the throat and yanked him towards her. She would've drained him in a heartbeat had Vanessa not interceded to save him once again.

"Wait, we might need him!" she said, dragging Sebastian away from Angel's outstretched fangs.

"Get off him bitch!" Angel objected but Henry agreed with the logic and sided with Vanessa.

"No, she's right. Leave him be," he said, feeling the Duke's presence in his decision.

"Fuck you, Henry. You don't get to tell us what to do just because the Duke is gone!" Angel hissed, outraged at Henry's audacity. She liked Henry and would've naturally sided with him 99 out of 100 (as long as it didn't affect her) but he had no right to stop her from doing what came naturally.

71

"Just until we know what we're dealing with," Henry conceded, giving Angel a face-saving way out which she reluctantly took. "After that he's all yours."

When Alice also urged Angel to exercise restraint, Angel could tell which way the mood was swinging and holstered her fangs.

"Fine," she shrugged. "I'll stick him downstairs with the others."

Vanessa grabbed Sebastian too and told Angel she would take him, which came with its own set of problems.

"I think it's best if I took him, don't you?" Henry finally said.

"But I brought him here tonight," Vanessa objected.

"I'll split him with you if you like?" Angel proposed, momentarily giving Vanessa pause for thought.

Sebastian didn't know what to make of it all as he was pulled this way and that. The prospect of a gruesome and bloody death left him shaken to the core. On the other hand if he did have to die tonight (and it seemed like he did) having Angel and Vanessa going twos-up on him as a method wasn't without its merits.

"Let go of him, both of you!" snapped a voice from the far side of the room. Angel and Vanessa turned in surprise to see Boniface glaring at them both.

"You're taking Henry's side now!" Angel exclaimed, and even Henry was having trouble believing this. Truly the world had gone mad.

"No sides, no arguments. Not if we're to get out of here tonight," Boniface said, for once taking the centre ground if only to see how it felt. Henry acknowledged Boniface's support with a grateful nod and decided to get Sebastian away from the girls before temptation could strike again. But before he could, Sebastian had a question of his own.

"Here, hang on a minute, what others?"

Henry didn't stop to explain. It was easier to simply show him so he marched Sebastian down to the cellar, across a pile of dead soldiers, and directed him towards a couple of chairs, both of which were currently occupied. The Thatchers gawped up at

72

him in fear and mouthed anguished pleas from behind their gags. They didn't like being tied up. Let's face it, who did? But the Thatchers in particular knew what happened to people who found themselves tied up – especially in this cellar.

"Who are they?" Sebastian asked as Henry plonked him into a chair of his own and wrapped some ropes around him.

"The Thatchers," Henry told him. "It's their farm."

Sebastian turned to Mr Thatcher nearest and nodded cordially at him. "Alright, how's it going?"

Mr Thatcher could only blink in response. Even if he'd not been tied and gagged he would've still probably just blinked. What a thing to ask!

Henry was greatly amused. And even little impressed. Sebastian had spirit. That went a long way with Henry. He was glad they'd let him live. If only for the time being.

"You know what, Sebastian, Vanessa was right about you. You really are something else," he told him.

Sebastian just about managed to rasp his lips and replied, "Coming from!" before Henry snuffed out that sentiment with a gag.

Upstairs, Chen and the others were looking over the equipment First Squad had gifted them. They'd seen a great many firearms in their time, albeit usually from the wrong end, but First Squad's lightweight carbine assault rifles were the very latest thing. Chen examined one of the rifles closely, identifying the trigger, the cartridge case and the hole it was advisable not to suck on whilst playing with the trigger, but there were other catches and buttons too, most of which he was less familiar with.

"Anyone used one of these before?" he asked.

Off in the corner, Alice ejected her cartridge case, caught it before it hit the floor, slammed home another and locked and loaded as if she were handling a new ball of wool.

"I've got one at home," she explained when she saw everyone looking at her in surprise. She might not have been able to work a DVD but when it came to dishing out death and destruction, few could match the sweet little old lady from Eastbourne.

CHAPTER 12

18 saw something he didn't understand at first. He adjusted the settings on his thermal image detector but there it was again. What was that?

The house was cold but the bodies of First Squad were still warm. Most had been deposited in the cellar and out of sight of the thermal image detector but one poor unfortunate, Private Stoker (otherwise known as 9), who'd tried to escape through an upstairs window, lay dead and disappointed with himself at the top of the stairs. 18 had noticed him earlier, just after the initial assault, but now he appeared to be moving again. Was he still alive? Should they attempt a rescue?

But his movements were odd. He didn't seem to be moving, simply jerking, again and again and again. What was happening to him?

"Sir," 18 said, calling to Colonel Bingham for a second opinion.

"What is it?" Colonel Bingham replied.

"Something odd," 18 told him, handing his superior the thermal image detector to see for himself.

Alas Private Stoker was indeed dead. As dead as dead could be in fact. But he was still very tasty – to some.

Boniface came trip-trapping up the stairs and caught Angel with her face buried into the former soldier's soft and sticky parts, blissfully indifferent to the Mephistophelian *faux pas* she was committing by feeding on the dead. This was a human habit, devised by barbarians and practiced by peasants. The Coven feasted only on the living. It wasn't just about the taking of blood. It was about the feasting on their food's life force. In vampiric terms, Angel was behaving no better than a tramp scoffing chips off the floor.

"Oh for God's sake, that's disgusting, stop that before the others see you," Boniface implored her.

"I don't care, I'm starving," Angel snarled back, her face sticky from Private Stoker's juices.

"But he's dead for God's sake. That's not right."

Angel raised an eyebrow. "But he's still warm. Want some? You know you do."

Boniface leaned against the banisters and didn't know whether to laugh or honk as Angel set about the carcass once more. Despite only seeing his friends once or twice a century he thought he knew them quite well but it was really only in the face of adversity that you got to know your peers. They had six or seven hours until the dawn trapped them here for good. What would happen once the sun started to poke up through the trees on the Eastern slopes. He'd seen people do terrible things in Stalingrad in the final hours of the siege, both to friends and foe alike. What would fate find them doing come 4.30am tomorrow morning?

Boniface had no chance to consider the question further. All at once the window at the top of the stairs shattered into a thousand pieces as a hail of lead ripped through the glass and into Angel's chest. The force of the impact drove her back against the far wall and tore her clothing to ribbons.

Boniface managed to duck the worst of the onslaught but was showered in glass and plaster as the side of the building was raked with gun fire.

As quickly as it had begun, it ended, leaving Angel battered, tattered and sore, and more than a little aggrieved.

"What the fuck was that for?" she said, climbing to her feet and brushing the bullets from her body as her innards closed up to squeeze them out.

"Someone else objecting to your questionable culinary habits, I would say," Boniface suggested with an unsympathetic smile.

"Everyone's a food critic these days," Angel glared, grabbing Private Stoker's assault rifle and taking up a defensive position at the newly created hole in the window.

Downstairs they'd heard the shots and thought they were a prelude to a second assault. When it didn't come Alice figured she would take the fight to the enemy, traded her assault rifle for a heavy duty M60 and headed for the door.

"Where's she going?" Chen asked as he watched her leave.

Vanessa didn't know but she knew to take cover all the same. Something was about to happen. And it wasn't going to be something good.

Alice flung open the front door and stepped out into the night. She scanned the hillsides and saw distant movement in the trees. She couldn't make out specifics, just silhouettes running amongst shadows, but she saw enough of them to turn on her heels.

"Eat this… you sons of bitches!" she beamed, squeezing the trigger to rake the treeline with a torrent of death.

Bingham and the others had seen Alice emerge. She'd moved pretty gingerly for a old lady so they'd not worried about her too much but now they were diving behind every trunk and hollow as Alice's firestorm chewed up the forest around them.

"For God's sake, nail that shooter somebody," Bingham ordered, giving his entire unit the order to fire at will.

The valley lit up with muzzle flashes as fire was poured onto the farm. North and south, east and west: Alice scanned the hillsides and counted at least forty-five points of fire before she was knocked back to the front door by a hail of lead.

Chen and Vanessa smashed their guns through the glass and covered Alice's retreat. She made it back to the farmhouse and ducked inside as the doorframe was blown apart around her.

Some people had no respect for their elders, she lamented sadly. Such was the way of the world.

Angel joined the impromptu fire fight, shooting from the top window and into the line of muzzle flashes several hundred yards away. She wasn't the best of shots, none of them were, as the Coven did their killing up close and personal (as God intended), but if she could knock one or two hats off one or two heads it might give the enemy something to think about.

By contrast Boniface made no attempt to enter the fray. He merely retired to a quiet corner to sit out the battle, as was his want. Boniface was not a fan of war. He'd seen too much of it in his time. If he'd been human he might've been irrevocably scarred by now but Boniface had simply grown indifferent. It never seemed to end. The pitiful reasons changed from century to century but the wars themselves were almost indistinguishable from one another. Lots of killing, lots of destruction and lots of suffering, more often than not felt not by the people who'd started these things but those without the means to escape them. This was mankind's real disease. And like so many of the worst diseases around, it was entirely self-inflicted.

But Boniface was alone in his objections. The others were quite happy to fight it out. Not least of all Angel who emptied an entire cartridge into the night without the foggiest idea who or what she was killing. If indeed she was even killing anyone. She might've just been shooting a bunch of cats' eyes for all she knew. It would've made no difference to her.

Like Alice, Bingham counted the points of fire coming from the farmhouse and saw four so far. This was more than he had expected but not as many as he had feared.

One of the lights to his left exploded in a pall of smoke and sparks. Another cut out further along the hillside and Bingham watched as the firing points in the farmhouse shifted further west.

"Cut the lamps," Bingham ordered. "They're going after the lamps."

The valley now plunged back into darkness to save the lamps from being shot out. Bingham would use them sparingly, only if the enemy attempted to make a break for it, and rely instead on their infrared gear from now on.

Alice kept going with the big gun, fanning the flames of the fight so that no one dared lay down their weapon.

"Alice? Alice?" Vanessa pleaded with her but Alice was just getting started.

"I'm busy," she snapped, concentrating her fire on one particular muzzle flash after another until it stopped flashing in her sights.

Down in the basement, Henry had no gun of his own. They'd all been left upstairs and he'd missed the part of the meeting where they'd voted to re-enact World War Two. He settled for poking his head up out of the coal chute now and again to see how the match was going. A shower of brick dust from a near miss advised him to duck again and he noticed Sebastian's expression as he brushed the grit from his shoulders.

"Glad you came?" Henry smiled.

Sebastian murmured an inaudible reply from behind his gag so Henry loosened it to allow him to talk.

"What was that?" he asked.

"I said oh yeah, vampires with machine guns; what's not to love?"

A ricochet down the coal chute, off the floor and up Henry's armpit underlined the point and made him wonder why people without an imperviousness to bullets would ever fire these things at one another.

Angel similarly took her second mauling of the evening, taking two to the head and one to the tits as she tumbled back against the same door she'd hit only minutes earlier.

"Fuck!" she swore jumping to her feet. "They got me again!"

"Yep," replied Boniface impassively, as if she were trying on dresses for his consideration, not fighting for their lives.

"There are other guns you know," Angel pointed out.

"I think you're all making quite enough noise without me," Boniface replied.

"Prick!" Angel snapped, but like sticks, stones and .45 calibre bullets, names could not harm Boniface.

*

Mr Larousse could hear the battle raging away on the other side of the forest and feared the worst. What had happened to Colonel Bingham's plan to contain them until sunrise? Why were they shooting? What was going on?

"Colonel Bingham, come in. I repeat, what's happening? Over. Talk to me," Larousse demanded.

The radio finally crackled to life and Colonel Bingham voice tickled his ear, together with a lot of tinny gunfire.

"They're trying out the weapons you gifted them, Father. Over."

It was a dig. Larousse knew it was a dig but he chose to rise above it. He had more important things to think about anyway. They all did. He could not allow himself to be drawn into petty squabbles with the Colonel.

"Stop firing! Stop firing! You're just wasting ammunition. You can't kill them that way anyway," Larousse told him.

78

"Maybe not, but they don't like it up them either," Colonel Bingham retorted, snatching up his own assault rifle and taking a bead on one of the lower window muzzle flashes.

Vanessa felt the Colonel's bullets tear into her. She landed in a heap and winced at the searing pain. She hated getting shot. It was an occupational hazard and something that happened from time to time but she'd still never got used to it.

"You okay?" Chen asked her when he saw her grimacing in the pain.

"I'll live," she replied.

Chen smiled: "True enough," before getting back to work.

The Thatcher's ramshackled old farmhouse was coming apart at the seams under the ceaseless assault, with brick dust and plaster filling the air to highlight the bullet trails zipping in through the broken windows. Several large cracks now raced around the walls and across the ceiling as the building seemed to drop to its knees.

Vanessa ducked beneath the table as a large chunk of artex fell from the ceiling and smashed to pieces all around her. Much more of this and they'd be returning fire from a pile of rubble.

Alice made it back into the farmhouse, ducking inside the house just as the doorframe behind her exploded to matchwood. The splinters sprayed in all directions to pepper her skin but she barely winced. She'd taken six bullets already and hadn't even lowered her gun. The .45 rounds she'd soaked up were nothing compared to the varicose veins she'd had to endure these last eight centuries.

Alice swung the machinegun out of the door and pulled the trigger again. There was something reassuring about how much the big dog kicked when it barked. More bullets came tearing back in reply but Alice didn't let up, not until the last of her ammo belt had raced through the gun to leave her standing in a pile of spent shells.

Alice chucked the gun and picked up an SMG. She was about to continue her one-woman assault when Vanessa called out to her to stop.

"Hold it. Wait a minute. Alice wait!"

Alice did as she was told, although it took all of her restraint to stop. But when she had, she heard what Vanessa had already heard.

Silence.

"They've stopped shooting," Angel said, holding her fire in the window at the top of the stairs.

Boniface brushed the dust from his jacket sleeve and let out a sigh of relief. "Thank God. I'm not sure my suit could've taken much more of that."

"You're not much fun in a fight, you know," Angel sneered. Boniface didn't care. He was bulletproof, both metaphorically and literally. His chance would come and when it did he would be ready. Until then he was on a permanent fag break.

Colonel Bingham had told his men to cease fire twenty seconds earlier. He'd lost three more men in the ensuing gun battle for no discernible gains. Larousse was right about one thing; they couldn't kill their targets with conventional weapons but hopefully they'd stung them enough to dissuade them from venturing out again.

"All we need to do is keep them there for the rest of the night. Just keep them contained. And the sun will do the rest in the morning."

18 hoped the Colonel was right. He felt as though he were caught between a rock and a hard place with the vampires on one side and the fanatical Mr Larousse on the other. He and his comrades were the middle men in the deal – here for the money but hanging on for their lives.

"Chin up 18, they must almost be out of ammo by now," the Colonel said.

"Them too?" 18 replied. "Thank fuck for that, I thought it was just me."

18 set down his smoking weapon and picked up his thermal image detector. Far below, in the doors and windows of the distant farmhouse, 18 picked out at least four guns glowing red on the display.

"There's four of them," he confirmed.

"No 18, there's a minimum of four of them," the Colonel Bingham corrected him. "Let's not keep making that same mistake, yeah?"

Bingham was right to be on his guard. Neither Boniface nor Henry had fired a shot all night and were therefore invisible to 18's heat detector. But while it was Boniface's apathy that was keeping him cloaked, Henry reasons for not engaging in the previous killing contest were somewhat more complicated. He retained a sense of morality, empathy even, for humans that the others found hard to understand. He had his needs and he wanted to live for as long as he could – if you called this living – but he wouldn't do so at any price.

He'd been a man of principles in his previous incarnation as an ordinary daylight dweller. And he saw no reason for that to change just because he had been forced to linger in the shadows.

Sebastian felt something wet on his chest and looked down to see his torso covered in blood.

"Oh shit! Oh shit, I've been shot!" he yelped, both horrified and a little impressed at himself for not even feeling it. God he was hard, wasn't he?

Henry looked down to see Sebastian rocking back in his chair at the sight of his own blood stained chest.

"What's the matter?" Henry asked, all matter-of-fact, as if Sebastian could have few grounds for complaint.

"What d'you think, you great fucking Helen Keller! I've been shot. Get us an ambulance, quick!" Sebastian said, half-panicking half-insulting without even trying.

"Relax, it's my blood," Henry reassured him. "You're fine."

Sebastian stopped struggling but felt no less easy. "Your blood?" he said with an grimace.

"Yeah look," Henry confirmed, showing him a gash in the side of his neck where he'd taken a ricochet to the jugular. Messy but, in Henry's case, non-fatal.

Sebastian began recoiling even more and demanded that Henry untied him.

"Please, just help me! Help me!" he implored, knocking into Mr Thatcher one way and then the mop and bucket the other as he fought to shake himself free from his sticky shirt.

"What's is it now?" Henry asked with neither compassion nor exasperation. Sebastian was merely a curiosity to him, to be tolerated out of courtesy.

"Well if it's your blood, mate, who knows what you've got," Sebastian outlined, imagining all sorts of micro monsters crawling all over his skin.

Henry didn't understand. As a night-feeder blood didn't trigger the same reaction in him as it did in modern men. There were no disposable rubber gloves in his world. Gore was good. Blood was life.

"What I've got?" Henry asked.

"Yeah no offence, chief, but it must go with the territory."

The penny finally dropped and Henry realised what Sebastian was getting at. The dreaded lurgy. The disease that had no cure. The ultimate curse.

"Sebastian, if I've got anything, it'll be Foot-and-Mouth-Disease, nothing more."

"Huh?" Sebastian huhhed.

Henry decided to come clean. His own kind might've looked down on him for his practices but he felt no shame in admitting the truth to Sebastian. "I'm not a human feeder. I only take from animals."

Sebastian was much confused. Not an uncommon state of affairs for him but this situation was different. Henry was unusual for a vampire.

"But I thought..." Sebastian started to say, only for Henry to cut him off.

"As most people do. But we don't all feed on humans. And I choose not to."

Mr and Mrs Thatcher glanced at each other in the darkness. They weren't sure what this meant in terms of their chances but surely this could only be a good thing. After all, if you had to be trussed up like a turkey in your own basement, who would you rather stood over you with the carving knife? Bernard Matthews or Linda McCartney?

But Sebastian failed to see the angle and asked why not.

Henry plucked a cigarette from his top pocket, wiped the blood from it and took a long lingering drag after lighting up. "Because I used to be one," he explained, before exhaling from half a dozen new blowholes, courtesy of the Colonel.

CHAPTER 13

"How many do you see?" Henry asked when he returned from the cellar.

Vanessa was crouching low at the kitchen window and scanning the horizon through her assault rifle's telescopic sights. It was difficult to discern much through the sights. They were fitted with night vision technology but then again so was Vanessa so the effect was somewhat disorientating, like looking through a child's kaleidoscope only with a super-bright torch sticking down the other end. "Enough," she concluded, lowing the rifle and rubbing her eye.

"Enough for what?" Chen felt the need to ask.

"Enough to stop us leaving before dawn," Vanessa clarified.

Chen thought on that for a bit then asked the obvious question. "What then?"

"Then, my dear boy, we won't be leaving at all," Alice told him, only too aware of the consequences of being trapped by daylight.

This was a vampire's worst nightmare. Being discovered by day. At night they could fight, they could move and they could kill. But by daylight all they could do was take cover and try to stay in the deepest darkest shadow. Even reflected light – the light that bounced off floors, ceilings and walls – could sear them like a hot lamp. But direct sunlight was the worst. It would burn them like a flame, boil their blood and ignite them in a flash so that they burnt to cinders. It was the worst and most agonising of deaths for a vampire and every member of the Coven rightly feared it. Even above death itself.

There was an old legend about a French vampire from the Middle Ages who'd had three daughters, each of whom carried his blood in their veins. They'd hunted across a vast territory, taking only from the sick and lame in the hope that their presence might be tolerated and for several centuries they were. But then one day the Marquis de Rouen's daughter fell ill. So distraught was the Marquis that he let it be known that he

84

would do anything to save his daughter, even if that meant selling his soul to the Devil. The chief vampire heard of the Marquis's plight and offered him a deal: they would grant his daughter the gift of eternal life if he would pardon them for their past crimes and promise never to hunt them again. It was deal like no other and it offered the vampires the one thing they'd always dreamt of – acceptance.

The Marquis agreed all too quickly and thus the chief vampire mixed his blood with the stricken girl's and within an hour she was walking, talking and laughing again after being all but dead. It was as if the Lord himself had delivered her from the grave. The vampires had made good on their word and now the Marquis made good on his, issuing a proclamation stating that the vampires were now under his protection: no man nor woman could harm them on pain of death. From this moment forwards they were safe.

The Marquis even came up with the novel idea of killing two birds with one stone by driving a cartload of condemned prisoners to their once secret keep at the end of every month so that the general population might be spared their nightly hungers. It was a fantastic deal and good for both sides.

Unfortunately it could not – and did not – last.

Once reborn, the Marquis's daughter was not content to feast on murderers and vagabonds as the father vampire and his daughters were. She had a more refined palette and preferred the richer bouquet of the province's aristocrats. The Marquis tried to curb his daughter's appetites but when the Mayor of Chartres's son was found dead in his bed he realised his efforts had been in vain. She could no longer be reasoned with because – as the Marquis saw it – she was no longer his daughter, but a foul creature of unspeakable evil.

Just as those he'd struck his Faustian pact with were also.

The Marquis put an end to his daughter's curse by driving a stake between her ribs, removing her head and burying her remains beneath a great marble slab inscribed with a warning for future generations not to disturb her rest.

But he showed no such leniency towards those who'd condemned her to eternal damnation. He took a hundred men to

85

their castle keep first thing in the morning and clamped them in irons as they slept. The chief vampire threw himself at the mercy of the Marquis and begged him to not to expose his daughters to the light. He'd been the one to infect the Marquis's daughter. He alone should be the one to suffer the unthinkable.

But the Marquis was a vindictive man and dragged them into the sun one-by-one so that each of them could witness the full horrors of what was about to befall them. The chief vampire died last, knowing that it had been his folly that had condemned his daughters to the ultimate agonies.

Henry couldn't remember who'd told him that legend but he remembered the fear he'd felt when he'd first heard it. It was the same white fear he now felt as he looked out of the window and up at the ridge –

– at men who'd been sent by another vengeful Marquis.

CHAPTER 14

Sebastian had been twisting his wrists over and over until he felt he'd worked a little slack into his bonds. Unfortunately, at the same time, the rope chafing had caused his wrists to swell so that he was not only no nearer to escaping, he was now in considerable discomfort.

He glanced over his shoulder and saw the iron leg of the workbench just behind him. It was peeling and rusty. If he could shunt a couple of feet backwards he might be able to rub his ropes against the corroded metal to free his hands.

Sebastian tried bouncing in his chair but didn't move. He bounced a bit harder and bumped into Mr Thatcher.

"Excuse me," Sebastian said but Mr Thatcher didn't reply. He couldn't. He and Mrs Thatcher still had their gags in whereas Henry had neglected to replace Sebastian's.

Sebastian bounced again and then again, slowly and agonisingly, clattering his way across the cellar floor until he was almost within reach of the rusty leg. One more bounce and he'd be there but in his excitement he lost his balance and keeled over sideways, crashing into the floor face-first to knock himself and couple of teeth out for several minutes. When he came to he discovered he could move his arms. In fact he was completely free. The chair had disintegrated around him when he'd hit the floor, releasing him from his ropes and his predicament.

"I did it," he told the Thatchers as if he'd just performed a Harry Houdini trick of careful design. "You see that? I did it."

The Thatchers nodded approvingly but this turned to protestations when Sebastian went to climb out of the coal chute without releasing them too.

"Don't worry, I'll come back with help," he reassured them. "Every second counts."

This just made Mr and Mrs Thatcher object even more vehemently and Sebastian thought he made out the word "motherfucker" in between Mr Thatcher's muffled grunts. He knew deep down that he should free the pair of them but the thought of lingering chilled Sebastian to the bone. Henry and the others could return at any second and that would be that, his one and only chance to get away would be gone. It might not have been the noblest course of action he was pretty sure he could live with himself all the same.

Mr and Mrs Thatcher continued to scream at Sebastian from behind their gags, so much so that he feared they'd alert their captors upstairs before he could escape. Resigned to taking the Wurzels with him he climbed down from the coal chute and stepped behind Mrs Thatcher.

"Fine, but you owe me," he told her, yanking down her gag.

"You can have a Victoria Cross and a nosh if you like, just get us the fuck out of here!" Mrs Thatcher replied peevishly, albeit quite understandably so.

*

Colonel Bingham had things on his mind too. Most people do when there's a bunch of gun-toting supernatural beings nearby intent on breaking out and killing everything in sight, but curiously the Colonel's thoughts had nothing to do with this.

Or at least not directly.

He was pondering the price of loyalty. Could a mercenary ever truly be considered loyal? He had fought all over the world, for banana dictators and freedom fighters alike, occasionally at the same time, but he had always done so for money.

Money was the key to Colonel Bingham's heart. Some mercenaries fought for the buzz and some for the cause but the Colonel had always looked at the pay packet first and the objectives second. Larousse paid well. Extremely well in fact. And up until tonight the job had been safer than guarding a homework shop on Christmas Day. It was the nest-feathering job to end all nest-feathering jobs.

And, of course, complete bonkers.

But the Colonel was happy to go along with it just to see his bank account fatten up. And it made a lovely change to be working in England after so many years abroad.

But then while on leave one weekend, the Colonel had been approached whilst feeding the ducks on Hampstead Heath. How this person knew who the Colonel was or what his mission concerned, he could only guess, but he'd even more money than Larousse and made the Colonel an offer he could not refuse –

– nor indeed fulfil.

Until tonight.

The creatures in the farmhouse were a plague to Larousse. But to others they were an opportunity. The Colonel pondered this thought in the darkness, as he sat on the ridge and stared out across the valley and into the abyss – in more ways than one.

The Colonel heard Larousse before he saw him. The rustling of leaves and cracking of twigs gave him away a full twenty seconds before anyone saw him. It could've only been Larousse. The Colonel's men moved silently through the forest. Larousse wouldn't have lasted five minutes in the Congo.

"Feeling brave, Mr Larousse?" the Colonel said, speaking up to help his employer find him in the darkness.

"I can't see anything from back there. I need to know what's happening," Larousse replied.

"Not much for the time being," the Colonel informed him. Indeed, all was quiet on the Western Front. The targets hadn't tried to move and the Colonel was content to leave them where they were. Stalemate.

Larousse squinted down at the farmhouse so Colonel Bingham handed him his binoculars.

"Thank you."

The Colonel watched Larousse as he studied the location. He was like a Peeping Tom in the bushes outside a Mastectomy Clinic. How could something so wrong feel so right?

"Can we hold them until sunrise, Colonel?" Larousse asked.

"If we don't, I'll be sure to let you know," the Colonel promised him.

Larousse ogled the farm some more. Was that a flicker of movement in the windows he saw? Was that one of them?

"They're really in there, aren't they? They're really just down there," he croaked. Larousse's throat was dry. Just like his outlook.

Bingham decided to test the waters with a suggestion of his own while he had Larousse to himself.

"What if we could take one of them alive?"

Larousse almost dropped the binoculars and looked at the Colonel in disbelief. Did he hear him right?

"What are you talking about?"

"Just to get a sample. Just for the sake of science," the Colonel probed, icing the cake to gauge his benefactor's reactions.

Larousse was outraged. After everything he'd tried to drum into these men and he should speak of science?

"These things are an abomination. They need to be wiped out, erased from the face of this Earth," Larousse sermonised. The spit had returned to his mouth with a vengeance and now threatened to douse the Colonel's collar.

"Righteous words, Padre. But could we be missing an opportunity here?" he smiled, brushing Larousse's flecks from his jacket, if only for effect. His jacket had seen far worse in its time. And no doubt would again tonight.

"We've got them trapped, Captain. This is our opportunity. We might never track so many of them down to one location again," Larousse harangued. He considered himself an open-minded individual. He had to, otherwise he wouldn't be here now. But some things were simply sacrilegious. Allowing even one of those creatures to live, even if it were muzzled and caged, was akin to harbouring Doctor Mengele from justice because he'd produced some interesting data in the death camps. "This is the chance of a lifetime."

Colonel Bingham pondered that last sentiment for a moment and found he agreed with it wholeheartedly. But for entirely different reasons.

"You're right," he told him.

"I know I am. And my authority comes from the very top," Larousse assured him, meaning not just the top dog on Earth but Him above too – if you believed in that sort of thing.

The Colonel pulled a dog-eared business card out of his pocket and nodded at one of his men crouched in the shadows just behind Larousse. Larousse heard the gun cock and felt its sights turned in him.

"Oh no no no no, you can't. What is this?" he demanded.

"My authority," the Colonel told him. "I'm in charge from now on."

CHAPTER 15

Down in the farmhouse things were no less fractious but at least no one was pointing their guns at anyone else. Their hackles were more than enough.

"Stay here then. See if we care. You're not one of us anyway!" Vanessa hissed at Henry by way of disagreeing with his last sentiment.

"I didn't say I wanted to stay here. I just said I wasn't going out there without a plan," Henry reasoned back. His colleagues might not have respected him for his feeding habits but they still listened to him. Henry didn't want to die any more than anyone else. On that they at least agreed.

"Let's just go for it. Make a run for the trees and go," Angel said, as if it was the most obvious thing in the world.

"Running's not a plan. Running's what you do when you don't have a plan," Henry pointed out.

The kitchen had been shot to pieces so they'd taken shelter under the stairs. The walls were thicker here, it was in the centre of the house and this part of the home had long been regarded as a bastion of sanctuary from outside harm. Why else had the Ministry of Defence in the 1980s recommended that people leant a door against the stairs to make a nuclear fall-out shelter in the event of a four-minute warning? It wasn't likely to protect anyone from an intercontinental ballistic missile strike but it gave the people a semblance of reassurance and kept the roads clear while Government officials raced for the real shelters.

Boniface remembered the Cold War as if it had been yesterday, which in his case it practically had been. He hadn't liked it. It had been his least favourite war so far, and this was coming from someone who despised all wars as a matter of course. But the Cold War was particularly repugnant: too much sneaking about, not enough carnage. What was the point of a war without some modicum of waste?

"Kismet catches everyone in the end. You can't run from it forever," Boniface said as he peered out of a bullet hole in the front door and up towards the ridge.

Angel disagreed. "Better to die roaring like a lion than bleating like a lamb."

"The whole place is surrounded," Boniface snorted with a shake of the head. "Just how far do you think you'll get anyway?"

"Far enough for my ashes not to get mixed up with yours will do just nicely," she replied.

"People, people," Henry urged them. They had enough to contend with already without tearing each other's faces off.

"I'm ready," Chen announced with steely-jawed determination.

"For what?" exclaimed Henry. "We haven't even decided what we're doing yet and you're already ready? Give us a chance, for fuck's sake!"

"Look, the game might be up for us but we can still make a few widows before this night's out," Angel said, flexing her talons around the handle of her assault rifle. Angel was psyched. She was a wolf on a leash just waiting to be released.

Angel hadn't felt this pumped in almost 130 years. Then it had been personal; her former familiar had crossed her and gone off on his own killing spree across Whitechapel, convinced that this would give him the gift without Angel's blessing. He'd managed to kill six times before she'd finally caught up with him. And when she did no one ever heard from Jack again.

"Of course we don't all have to get away, you know," Alice suggested with a knowing smile.

Vanessa wasn't sure she heard right. Was this some sort of drawing straws shit designed to help old granny get away. "What are you talking about, old woman?" she snapped irritably.

"I'm a hundred years younger than you," Alice took pleasuring in reminding Vanessa.

"And don't you look good for it," Vanessa replied, equally pleasured to remind Alice of that.

"Shut up both of you and stop bickering," Boniface said, when the penny dropped with him. "She's right."

"About what?" Vanessa said, now doubly irritated that Alice seemed to have seen something that had, thus far, eluded her.

Boniface explained. "As long as they've got us where they can see us we're hog-tied. But if just one of us can get clear, get to the shadows..."

"... the night is ours."

All eyes turned to Angel and now understood. The night was indeed theirs. No mortal man could outmanoeuvre them in the shadows. They could get behind their attackers, pick them off at will and create a panic which, in theory, would allow more of their rank to slip out and join the fray.

Henry nodded in approval and looked around.

"Okay okay, so now we've got a plan," he said.

"I'm ready," Chen agreed, his jaw still clenched in anticipation.

"There you go, Chen's ready," Henry sighed, rolling his eyes in exasperation. Some people couldn't wait to die, could they?

Angel cocked her gun even though it didn't need cocking. But she felt the occasion called for a gesture of machismo and was willing to waste a cartridge on theatrics. "So we break as one, in one direction, at the same time," she told her comrades.

Alice, the architect of the idea, also felt the need to demonstrate a show of strength and finally set her knitting needles down once and for all. "Then first one clear doubles back and butchers every last living one of them," she smiled sweetly.

*

Colonel Bingham had never called the number on the business card before. He'd been tempted, but he'd never had the need and he wasn't a man to waste other people's time. Their lives perhaps but never their time.

When he finally did call he had expected alarm bells and helicopters but all he got was a recorded message.

"*Thank you for calling. Please leave your name and circumstances after the tone and someone will get straight back to you,*" the message had told him.

"Fuckers!" the Colonel replied. Larousse's lips curled in the darkness but they didn't stay curled for long. No sooner had the Colonel hung up than his phone lit up again. He answered.

"Yes?"

Larousse watched the Colonel's conversation but gleaned very little.

"Yes. Yes. Maybe. Yes. Half a mile. More than four. No sooner than that? We'll be here. Roger. Over and out."

Colonel Bingham pocketed his phone and Larousse stepped towards him, although he was careful to do so as unthreateningly as possible, bearing in mind the assault rifles trained on his back.

"Who was that?" he demanded.

"Someone who pays more than you, Mr Larousse," the Colonel replied.

"Thirty pieces of silver is it?" Larousse scowled, much to the Colonel's amusement.

"More or less, and adjusting for inflation," he winked.

18 was happy to stay out of it. He was rank and file. Nothing more. Politics and mutinies were the prerogatives of the officer classes. All he wanted to do was keep the enemy at arm's length, watch his buddies' backs and make it out of here in one piece. Anything else was bacon and eggs to 18 and he would deal with that in the morning.

"Oh shit! We've got movement," he said, spotting a stirring in the shadows at the side of the farmhouse.

Colonel Bingham hurried to his side and aimed his binoculars at where 18 was pointing.

"What the hell is that?"

18 didn't know. But whatever it was it was big and gnarly and growing gnarlier by the second.

CHAPTER 16

"Oi watch it! I don't even let my husband put it up there!" Mrs Thatcher barked down the coal chute as Sebastian sought to shove her up it.

"Well use your arms as well then, I ain't a bleeding lift!" Sebastian replied, becoming better and better acquainted with her in ways that Mr Thatcher could only vaguely remember.

Snug wasn't the word (the coal chute that was) but Mrs Thatcher was determined to get out of that cellar one way or the other.

"Come on Frodo, put your back into it!" she urged her knight in shining armour, scrambling all over his head and kicking him in the face on the way out. She dropped out of the hole and rolled over in the frozen mud outside. The moon shone brightly above. She'd done it. She was free! She'd stared death in the face and had now been reborn. She felt exhilarated. Delirious even. Nothing could stop her except possible for…

CRACK!

A bullet pinged off the brickwork just inches from her head.

Mrs Thatcher screeched and hugged the mud.

CRACK!

Another shot. This one even closer.

Mrs Thatcher couldn't move. She was paralysed with fear. Out of the frying pan and into the fire. When would this nightmare end?

"Well get up then you lazy old cow. Go on, get out of here!" Sebastian urged her, popping his head up out of the coal chute to see what the delay was.

"But they're shooting at me!" Mrs Thatcher replied.

"Then zig-zag. Dodge and weave, you know, like in the films."

Mrs Thatcher steeled herself with a deep breath and jumped to her feet.

Unbeknownst to her, Colonel Bingham had already ordered his men to cease firing after 18 had confirmed she had a

96

heat signal with his thermal image detector and was therefore not one of their targets. But the farmer's wife stuck with the plan anyway and lumbered backwards and forwards in agonisingly slow loops across the open ground to the bemusement of all those watching.

"What is she doing?" the sniper on the southern ridge asked as he followed her with his crosshairs back and forth, back and forth, covering just about every blade of grass between them and the farm.

"Evading our fire, it seems," his spotter deduced.

"Well let's see if we can't give her a little encouragement then, shall we," the sniper said, squeezing his trigger three more times to splatter the ground around her and get her moving a little quicker.

"Ooohh aarhhh, dodge and weave, dodge and weave!" Mrs Thatcher shrieked in response, jumping this way and that to sidestep the danger as best she could.

The soldiers weren't the only ones to witness Mrs Thatcher's dash for freedom. Henry stood at the kitchen window and watched on dispassionately as one of their hosts stumbled and bumbled across the finishing line and into the trees at the top of the ridge.

"Trouble?" Angel asked as she appeared at his side.

"Possibly," Henry replied. "But not for us."

Sebastian saw Mrs Thatcher make it too and bounded up and down with glee as she completed her home run.

"I don't believe it. She did it. She made it!"

But Mr Thatcher, still wrapped up like a forgotten Christmas present and left unwanted in the corner of an old abandoned grotto, failed to share in the joy of his wife's blessed deliverance and swore at Sebastian from behind his filthy gag.

"Alright mate, don't look at me like that. She was the one who didn't want to wait for you, not me," Sebastian informed him before starting on Mr Thatcher's ropes.

*

The first soldier Mrs Thatcher tripped over grabbed her and took her to the Colonel for debriefing. Mrs Thatcher couldn't believe the hub of activity she found in the forest this night. As far as the eye could see – which in this light was admittedly not that far – there were soldiers crouching, scanning the grounds, patrolling the woods and communicating with each other as they kept a watch on the farm below. The cavalry had come in their hundreds. But then again they'd done so at Little Big Horn too.

The Colonel, now confidently chomping on a fat Cuban cigar, turned to greet Mrs Thatcher when she was brought to him.

"Oh thank you. Thank you. You don't know what I've been through," Mrs Thatcher wheezed, ratcheting up her feminine frailties a notch or two for the Colonel's benefit.

"Who are you?" Bingham asked.

"I live here. I'm Melissa Thatcher. They came tonight," she told him, trying to decide or not whether a tactical swoon might help at this point.

"How many of them are there?" the Colonel asked, nodding at the soldier beside her to hand her a little cup of coffee.

Mrs Thatcher accepted the offer gratefully and gulped it down before answering. The Colonel was perfectly happy to wait for her response.

"Six or seven maybe – and some ratty little scumbag. They're all in it together," she said, adding a little smoke to her answers to screen certain other facts that might come to light over the course of this evening. There were certain advantages to being the first away, namely that you could be the first to put your side of the story across. Mrs Thatcher was determined to capitalise on this advantage until a thought occurred to her. The only thing better than getting her side of the story across first was being the only one left with any sort of story to tell, so she looked at the Colonel and said; "Probably with my old man too, knowing him. He's mad he is. Dangerous as well. Someone has to stop him."

The Colonel scrutinised Mrs Thatcher carefully.

"Leave it with me," he said, laying a reassuring hand on her shoulder.

*

Mr Thatcher had shown Sebastian about as much patience as he could muster but now he was starting to annoy him. After four minutes of fiddling with his wrists all Sebastian had managed to do was somehow tighten the knots to crank up his discomfort. Now he'd turned his attention to the coils around his midriff and was trying to free Mr Thatcher by simply yanking them again and again to chafe his back to buggery.

"I can't get them off. They're done up too tight," Sebastian eventually concluded, stepping back for a fag and a think.

Mr Thatcher chewed on his gag as he tried to say something but Sebastian couldn't understand him.

"What?"

Mr Thatcher tried again, only this time with a lot more colour to his face and diatribe as he tried to direct this fuckwit to take off his gag.

"What?" Sebastian simply said again, prompting an all-out explosion of murderous frustration from Mr Thatcher. It was a good job his hands were tied because they would've been around Sebastian's throat by now if they hadn't been.

"Oh, hang on a minute, let me try something" Sebastian said, at last loosening Mr Thatcher's gag to let him speak. "Now, what was it you were saying?"

Mr Thatcher swallowed his rage. It would do him no good to berate Sebastian while he was still tied to this chair. But as soon as he was out of these ropes...

"Just cut the bloody things off. There's a knife over there on the work bench."

Sebastian looked about.

"What workbench?"

"Over there. That enormous great metal thing," Mr Thatcher told him, still trying to stay calm.

"That's a workbench?" Sebastian said in surprise. It looked more like a giant sluice tray, with a shallow basin design and plughole at the one end.

"Never mind about that. Just find the knife," Mr Thatcher urged him.

"I can't see one. Where is it?" Sebastian replied, much to Mr Thatcher's frustration who could see it plain as day.

"On the work bench you big blindo. Right in front of you!" he fumed, getting steadily angrier and angrier.

For reasons known only to Sebastian he started opening cupboards about him.

"What, in here?" he asked, systematically going through cupboard after cupboard but finding only rucksacks and hiking boots – lots of them.

"For God's sake, there, it's just there!" Mr Thatcher snapped, trying to point at the knife with his head but instead simply prompting Sebastian to open the big fridge in front of him.

"What, in here?" Sebastian said.

"No no no! Stay out of there!" Mr Thatcher shouted but it was too late. The door swung open, the light clicked on and the giant refrigerator revealed all.

Sebastian was still looking for a knife so he didn't see anything out of the ordinary at first. In fact, the light coming on had helped by making the knife glint on the edge of the workbench. He grabbed it and turned back to Mr Thatcher in triumph, expecting to see a smile of approval only to find a look of horror instead.

"What?" Sebastian said, looking back at the rows and rows of pickle jars in the fridge when they finally registered with him.

That's when he saw someone staring straight back at him. The head in a jar wore the same gormless expression as Sebastian although his was not an expression of confusion but regret at trying to save a few quid by hitchhiking home instead of taking the train. All about him were his hands, feet, heart and unmentionables, bobbing up and down in different jars along with a couple of other festival goers and a geography graduate on work experience with Ordinance Survey Maps.

"Nothing to do with me, sport. They were here when we moved in," Mr Thatcher said sheepishly.

*

100

Colonel Bingham had gleaned just about all the intel he could out of Mrs Thatcher and now had a clearer picture of what was going on inside the farmhouse.

"And you're sure that's everything, are you?" he said, fixing her with a warm but no-nonsense smile.

"Yes yes I told you, now please, let me go. I've a heart condition you know. I'm not a well woman," she pleaded, desperate to slip away before the manure hit the fan, as she knew it was about to.

Her debriefing had drawn quite an audience with Larousse and several others watching on with interest. Larousse was now convinced he'd hit the jackpot and had snared every vampire in the country with this operation. He knew roughly how many could operate over any given territory so the maths pointed to the obvious conclusion. In a way Larousse was heartened. No matter what the treacherous Colonel Bingham did tonight, they'd struck a blow against evil that would reverberate around the world. Larousse would be a hero. His reputation was assured. And so would Colonel Bingham's only in a different way. Larousse would see to that, come what may.

Colonel Bingham ushered Mrs Thatcher away from the farm and deeper into the trees. "Of course, my dear. Please, come this way."

But Mrs Thatcher didn't want an escort. All she wanted to do was unstick herself from this sticky situation and disappear just as she had always planned to do. She had a safety deposit box in Folkestone with enough money to live on comfortably for several years and the passport of someone who'd borne an uncanny resemblance to her she'd met along the way. Mrs Thatcher had kept it for just such an occasion. All she needed was a ten-minute head start and she'd be sunning herself in Albania before the week was out.

"Thank you Colonel, but I don't want to cause you no bother. I can find my own way from here," she said, side stepping the Colonel and heading off in a different direction.

Colonel Bingham once again placed a hand on Mrs Thatcher's shoulder, only this time his grip wasn't quite so reassuring. "I insist," he indeed insisted.

Mrs Thatcher felt an icy fear wash over her. The Colonel was going to slap her in chains; she knew it. She'd be found out. She'd have to answer for what she had done. Or rather, her horrible husband had done. Yes yes, she had to remember that. She'd had no choice but to go along with him otherwise she would've ended up like all the others. If it came to it that was the story she would tell but there was still a chance. The woods were dark and the Colonel had other fish to fry. Surely he wouldn't worry too much about a poor little old country girl who'd never done anything to anyone.

"Well, er… if I can just use that tree over there first," she said, pointing into the darkness away from the Colonel. "I have been tied up half the night. Bleeding busting I am!"

Mrs Thatcher hurried off the path and into the trees, hoping the Colonel would respect her privacy whilst she watered the bracken. She knew these woods like the back of her husband's head (the dirty old bugger) and knew she could give David Blaine a run for his money when it came to vanishing acts.

But the Colonel was not one to stand on propriety and followed Mrs Thatcher into the shadows. Taking out his sidearm as he went.

*

Mr Thatcher was still tied up in his chair as Sebastian started shimmying up the coal chute.

"Let me out! Let me out, you bastard! Cut these ropes!" he shouted but Sebastian was more inclined to go upstairs and ask Angel for a kiss than he was to free this fruitcake.

"And end up pickled like that lot? No thanks. You've got everything coming to you sunshine," Sebastian said, wishing him a fond farewell on behalf of the vegetable drawer who were unable to speak for themselves.

But Sebastian had clambered no more than a few feet up the chute when he heard a scream of terror that stopped him in his tracks, followed by the crack of a distant gunshot. Mrs Thatcher had left the building. Permanently.

Whoever she'd found out there had been just as dangerous as those upstairs. Sebastian was caught between a rock and a hard place, a frying pan and a fire, and death and damnation.

Samuel Johnson had really hit the nail on the head when he'd said, "When a man is tired of London he is tired of life". If this was what it was like in the sticks, the *Country Life* set could bloody keep it.

*

Up on the hill Colonel Bingham strode back out of the shadows alone, holstering his sidearm once more.

18 was aghast. He'd seen plenty of death in his time but the killing of civilians still appalled him. He would have no part of this and stepped out to berate the Colonel as he passed.

"What the hell did you do that for?" he asked. It may have escaped the Colonel's notice that they were in the middle of a forest but it hadn't escaped 18's. There was no end of trees to tie a prisoner to around here.

The Colonel didn't take umbrage with 18's reaction. He'd served alongside a great many principled soldiers in his time. Each man was entitled to a conscience although more often than not those that did still lay in the paddy fields and trenches the Colonel had made it out of simply because they'd not had the stomach to do what was necessary.

"She could've been in league with them," he explained with a pragmatic shrug.

"Could've? What sort of a justification is that?" 18 demanded.

"An uncertain one, 18. Now we have certainty."

"You're mad. This is madness," 18 exclaimed.

Colonel Bingham fixed 18 with his best Nuremberg stare and said; "This is war, 18. And you'd best decide which side you're on – before dawn."

*

Sebastian climbed down from the coal chute and examined his options. He could either get shot outside, eaten inside or pickled where he was. All things considered he should've probably known Vanessa was never into him for normal reasons. A woman like than and a lad like him? He should've stuck with the girl in the kebab shop. She might not have been much to look at

103

but at least she'd never tried to kill him. And she always gave him extra meat on the side. In more ways than one.

"We'd been together almost twenty years, her and me. She didn't deserve that," Mr Thatcher lamented, still tied where he had been all night, in his chair.

"I'm sorry," Sebastian said, genuinely meaning it. Even serial killers had feelings.

Mr Thatcher chewed his lip for a bit then appealed to the only person in the world who was in a position to help him. "Please, I'm asking you as one human being to another, cut these ropes and let me go."

Sebastian opened the fridge to look at Mr Thatcher's collection of backpackers and shook his head. "I'm sorry mate, I can't do that."

The sympathy angle exhausted, Mr Thatcher decided to try and different approach.

"Look, it wasn't me, honest. It was the wife. I loved her and but I couldn't stop her. Fucking nuts she was."

"Every marriage has its difficulties," Sebastian sympathised, pulling a cigarette out of his packet and slipping it between his lips.

"I should cocoa," Mr Thatcher agreed, putting it mildly. "So, will you let us go?"

Sebastian lit his cigarette.

"Nope."

At that moment a bullet streaked across the fields, hit the side of the barn, bounced into the coal chute and ricocheted around the cellar until it found a pair of testicles to obliterate. Fortunately for Sebastian they weren't his, but a pair Mrs Thatcher had been saving for later, but it made Sebastian's eyes water nevertheless as he was showered with white vinegar and broken glass.

"What now?" he said, as the gunfire started up again in earnest.

CHAPTER 17

Colonel Bingham had ordered his men to open fire immediately at the first signs of movement and the front door swinging open had reignited the hostilities.

The six surviving Coven members had dashed out to take cover in the front garden. The idea was to break as one, in one direction, and overwhelm their attackers until they breeched a section of line. If just one of them could get beyond the enemy and disappear, they could then double back and pick them off at will. They might not get them all but they would certainly get enough to allow the others to join the fray.

And then what?

And then it would be a free-for-all in the darkness and Henry and his friends would back themselves all night long with that kind of advantage.

Colonel Bingham was acutely aware of the dangers and ordered his men to converge on three sides and push them back into the house. The result was a firestorm of lead that whizzed and cracked all around the Coven's heads.

Henry crouched behind a roller that had been left to rust in the middle of the lawn and called to Angel who was sheltering behind a dead tree.

"*Once more unto the breach, dear friends? Once more.*"

Angel smiled and looked to Vanessa to her left who was hugging the slate wall. "*Or close up the wall with our English dead.*"

Vanessa nodded back. "*In peace there's nothing so becomes a man.*" She now looked to Boniface who was steeling himself behind a tin pigsty and urged him to pick up the baton.

Boniface looked back at her.

"What?"

Vanessa merely repeated her line. "*In peace there's nothing so becomes a man.*"

Boniface snorted and pulled a face. "I'm not doing it," he said, jumping out from behind the sty and charging up the hill. "Come on you bastards!"

"I told you," Angel said, shaking her head in sadness. "No fun and no sense of occasion."

They broke in twos, with Henry and Angel running for the stables while Vanessa and Chen made for the chicken sheds. They all knew to make for the big old skeletal oak tree silhouetted on the crest of the ridge and there they would fight their way through the soldiers, soaking up every bullet in their arsenal if need be but driving on. It would sting and it would slow them down but it wouldn't stop them.

Henry covered Angel with short bursts then ran ahead, only for Angel to return the compliment, and in no time at all they'd crossed much of the open ground between their attackers and the farm.

Vanessa and Chen were also making headway, with Chen leading the charge while Vanessa covered the rear. Two soldiers ran out of the darkness to intercept them and shot them through with both clips. Ordinarily this would've been enough to neutralise any enemy but Vanessa and Chen were only stung. They rolled in the mud screaming and cursing mortal man, then returned fire, knocking the heads off both as they sprinted in for the kill.

"Motherfuckers!" Vanessa hissed, shaking her hand to tensing her stomach muscles to squeeze the bullets out.

"Come on, there's more where that came from," Chen gasped, trying not to show his own pain to endow Vanessa with the strength to go on. Vanessa snarled in response and jumped to her feet.

"I'll kill them all," she seethed before once again pushing into the storm.

Colonel Bingham saw them coming every step of the way. Six points of fire moving fast, heading his way, and not stopping for shit.

"Second Squad, hold your positions. Don't let a single one of them out of your sights. Third Squad, you've got two to your left. Don't let them through. Use the crossbows," he said, radioing each position in turn as he reorganised his troops as the battle unfolded.

The first few bolts missed their mark but when Chen was struck in the neck he and Vanessa immediately realised the danger. They might've been able to run through a hail of lead but a crossbow bolt to the heart could put them down for good.

Chen pulled the bolt from his throat and snapped it to examine it. It was indeed made from hawthorn. Whoever these bastards were they knew their stuff.

"We've got to get back!" he warned the others but it was already too late. The bolts were flying in from all directions and Angel and Boniface had been skewered, though nowhere fatally.

"Move in," Larousse urged Colonel Bingham. "Take the fight to them."

Boniface was the first to turn and flee. The farm might've been a death trap but at least it didn't offer instant death unlike Alice's fool idea. He would take another couple of hours of life over a heroic death any day of the week so he turned on his heels and found running downhill was a lot easier than running up had been.

When he arrived back in the Thatcher's dung-ridden courtyard all was relatively quiet. He'd outrun the battle – again. And this gave him pause for thought.

The cars?

Boniface found them all neatly parked at the rear of the hayloft and untouched by war. The tracks might have been barricaded but he was fully insured and ready to sacrifice his no claims bonus to punch through to the main road. There was only one problem.

"Chen you asshole, where's our fucking keys?" he said, trying each car door in turn only to find it securely locked. When he got to Vanessa's Jag her alarm started wailing, giving fair warning of his intentions to all those outside.

"Bastard!" he swore, then caught a set of keys glinting inviting out of the corner of his eye – in the ignition of a dirt bike leaning up against the side of the barn. "Okay, that could work," he concluded.

Third Squad heard the dirt bike's engine crank up before they caught up with Boniface – just a little too late. He smashed straight through the rickety barn door, clobbering the point man in the process and spraying the others with gravel and horse droppings as he spun it in a donut and took off for the main road. Bullets whizzed past him and a crossbow bolt found his shoulder but he was soon out of range and going hell for leather.

Motorcycles were something new to Boniface. He'd ridden a few in his time and knew how to work the controls but having spent the first 2000 years of his life riding horses he couldn't shake the habit of tethering his bike once he'd got where he was going and wondering where to stuff in the oats.

The dirt track leading away from the farm was clear. Boniface looked back and saw the farm as just cluster of foreboding shadows in the distance. He was almost away, which raised another interesting thought in his mind. Did he stick with the plan and double back into the woods? Or did he keep going and leave his comrades to their fate? There were pros and cons to both ideas. The question was, which would serve Boniface best?

Unfortunately his thinking time had run out.

A line of powerful arc lamps lit up the track in front to dazzle him in the glare. Shouts and gunfire accompanied the wall of light and his front wheel hit a pothole to toss him from the saddle. Boniface landed in a hedgerow and for a moment he was caught on its thorns as boot steps rushed towards him. A whoosh of a crossbow bolt gave him all the motivation he needed to untangle himself and he hurried through the brambles, paying no heed to the thousands of barbs that sought to claw his face off.

The soldiers shot into the bush but Boniface was already through to other side and running across the field, casting a cross of dark shadows from the arc lamps that followed him wherever he went.

"Stop right there. We have you surrounded!" shouted one of the soldiers more in hope than in conviction but Boniface wasn't about to give himself up. He knew what happened to people who threw themselves at the mercy of the enemy. It had happened to everyone in his village two thousand years earlier but it wouldn't happen to him. When his time came Boniface would die on his feet not on his knees. Admittedly his feet might be pointing away from the fight but he'd be on them nevertheless. It was a point of principle with him.

Bullets and bolts chased Boniface through the night, across the field and into the shadows of the valley of death, and back to where he'd just come from.

*

Henry and Angel were faring no better. They found themselves pinned down on the hillside taking fire from all sides. The bullets took the wind out of their sails but it was the bolts they really feared.

Up until now they'd kept their attackers at bay with a constant salvo of fire but now their clips were running low.

"There's too many of them!" Henry said, squeezing his trigger to chew up the turf in between the blinking muzzle flashes moving around to his left.

Angel ducked as she felt her hair parted in several new places thanks to the enemy on the hill. "We're going to die out here," she agreed, returning the compliment only to find her gun clicking empty after just two rounds.

She counted her clips and found she had only a couple left, just enough to cover their retreat but not enough the renew their assault.

"Come on, let's go!" she told Henry, slapping him on the back and pointing back in the direction of the farm.

*

Mr Thatcher and Sebastian were likewise not enjoying the fireworks. Sebastian had reacted by taking shelter in the furthest corner of the cellar while Mr Thatcher's options were somewhat more limited, given that he was still tied in his chair and in plain view of the coal chute.

Several stray bullets snapped around the cellar to shower Mr Thatcher with bits of plaster and fuel his pleas for mercy. "Help me. Help me. For the love of God, help me!" he said over and over again, hearing Sebastian cowering beneath a bench somewhere behind him without being able to see him.

But Sebastian didn't trust Mr Thatcher, certainly not enough to untie him. But equally he couldn't do nothing. If he sat idle and let Mr Thatcher die that would be as good as killing

109

him himself – albeit without having to burn his clothes afterwards. It was clear that nobody within five miles of this farm had a conscience but Sebastian did and it drove him to risk his own life for Mr Thatcher.

Crawling forwards and into open ground, he waited for the latest ricochet to run out of zip before jumping up and shoving a filthy tin bucket onto Mr Thatcher's head.

"Best I can do, mate," he told him, quickly retreating back into his foxhole again.

"What good is this, you great nimrod?" Mr Thatcher objected angrily, although this question was answered with a clattering ding as the bucket came to his aid almost immediately. "Alright, I take all it back, that was quite helpful," Mr Thatcher admitted, although he did wonder why Sebastian had picked the pigs' slop bucket over the one he used to water the horse with.

*

Vanessa and Chen made it all the way back to the farmyard but they'd been followed by a detachment of Second Squad. The first Vanessa knew about it was when a bolt hit her in the back to dump her onher face. She rolled over and machine-gunned her assailant to Swiss cheese but others were already on their way.

Chen yanked the bolt from Vanessa's back to make her roar in agony.

"Sting a bit, does it?" Chen deduced.

"Just a smidge," Vanessa confirmed through gritted teeth.

But now Chen found this out for himself as a flurry of arrows found their mark when the rest of Second Squad caught up with the pair of them.

Vanessa and Chen emptied their guns into this renewed assault but the soldiers kept on coming. All they'd done was buy themselves some time.

"Go! Get out of here!" Chen urged Vanessa, soaking up more shafts in order to protect his friend.

Vanessa refused to leave but Chen recognised a hopeless situation when he saw one and he used all of his strength to shove her away; away from the bolts, away from the approaching soldiers and away from him as he prepared to meet his maker.

Vanessa's stumble turned into a run and soon she found herself going for broke in the other direction. She loved Chen with all of her heart but like every night feeder she was first and foremost a lone wolf. And her instincts to survive soon kicked in.

Chen watched her go then jumped to his feet. As the Coven's security officer he couldn't help but feel a tad responsible for tonight's unexpected visitors. Of course he couldn't have known or prevented it from happening but like the Captain of the *Titanic* he felt it was his duty to see his friends to the lifeboats first. And equally, like Captain Smith a hundred years earlier, he was still secretly hoping to find a great big fucking sandbank just beneath his hull to save his hat from getting wet. But as more and more soldiers rushed in from all sides Chen knew it wasn't to be. Twelve hundred years of night were about to come to an end.

But he wasn't going out without a fight.

The first arrow grazed his cheek as he ducked to avoid it. The second buried itself into his shoulder but he pulled it out and hurled it back into the eye of the soldier who'd fired it.

More arrows soon followed but the kevlar armour Chen had lifted off First Squad shielded his vulnerable heart and his movement protected him further.

"Shoot him in the sides, between the vests," Second Squad's leader told his archers, but Chen just jumped, spun and pirouetted between their fields of fire to remain unharmed.

Bullets raked his body but Chen was now impervious to pain. All he wanted to do was kill as many of his attackers as he could and set out his stall by grabbing the leader and snapping his neck like a twig before anyone else could blink.

Soldiers to the left and right broke ranks and Chen seized the opportunity to pick them off with ease, even whilst soaking up more arrows. He bit one, ripped another's throat out with his bare hands and used the last one as a shield to give his own body a brief respite from all the bullets.

"Move it, go that way!" the lead crossbow archer told his fellow bowmen. "Stay out of his reach!"

The way Chen tore the head from the soldier he held provided all the motivation they needed and they fanned out either side of the wounded vampire to try to get one clean shot of his unprotected midriff.

Chen snarled with laughter when he saw the fear in his enemy's faces. The tide was turning. The fight was swinging his way. One of the bowmen broke and deserted, preferring dishonour to death, leaving Chen facing just two others, each with only a handful of bolts left.

"Take him! Take him! Take him!" the furthest urged the nearest but the nearest complained he didn't have a shot.

Chen leapt, not at the nearest but the furthest, to take him by surprise. He snatched him cleanly, grabbing his weapon in the process and killing the soldier opposite before he could get a shot off. Now only one of Second Squad remained and he was pinned to the ground with Chen's fangs bearing down on him.

"Help me! Help me, for the love of God!" Private Woodcock screamed, terrified beyond even his wildest comprehensions.

"God has forsaken you," Chen chuckled into the Private's ear as he bit down on his neck and sucked deeply on his rich, salty gore.

An arrow to the top of the head hurt like hell and Chen looked up just in time to see the deserter return, bringing with him vital reinforcements from Third Squad. Chen launched himself at them but he was too late. He'd let his guard down for the briefest of seconds and that was all the bowmen needed.

Twin arrows struck him in either side skewering his heart with surgical precision. He'd never known an agony like it but his screams were cut short as a machete took off his head. It landed with a thump to stare into the eyes of Private Woodcock, who'd never believed in God before this moment but who was now born again in every sense.

"Thank you, thank you," he told his rescuers, scrambling away from Chen's crumbling head and backonto his feet. He clutched his tattered neck and felt the ooze of his own blood seeping between his fingers but it wasn't a deep cut. He would live to fight another day and make the bastards pay for what they'd done to his friends. "Get me a bandage," he said, reaching out for a supporting hand from his comrades.

His comrades stepped back.

"Sorry bro, nothing we can do for you," one of them replied, raising his crossbow and firing a bolt into Private Woodcock's heart. The Private died in an instant, with his soul stained for all eternity to ensure he wouldn't be meeting his newly acquired Saviour after all.

CHAPTER 18

Vanessa got as far as the outhouses. Third Squad had pursued up to block off the perimeter and now she found herself caught out in the open, just as Chen had been.

She didn't know what had happened with Chen but Third Squad sure as hell did and they were reluctant to take on another target at close quarters. But if they could hem her back, ward her away from the woods and keep her penned into the farm where they could keep track of her, the sun would do their work for them in a few short hours.

A crossbow bolt struck the side of the barn just in front of where Vanessa was running, prompting her to turn and double back again. More soldiers were now pouring out of the darkness and Vanessa saw no way out until she noticed the chicken shed to her right. The door was invitingly ajar and she figured she could either take shelter inside or break out of the other. A second crossbow bolt striking close still made up her mind once and for all so she slipped into the shed and pulled the door shut quietly behind her.

"Squawk! Squawk! Cluck and Screech!" the birds all yelled in unison, only too adept at recognising a predator when they sensed one.

Vanessa turned and bared her fangs in irritation and put a finger to her lips. "Shhhhh!" she commanded and in that instant the shed fell silent, save for half a dozen hastily delivered eggs being scrambled on the floor.

Now that the chorus line had sat down, Vanessa was able to turn her ears to what was going on outside the shed. Boots ran this way and that, circling the shed and taking up positions, yet no one attempted to get too close. Vanessa decided to take this as a good sign – at least until she peered through a crack in the door and saw two soldiers crouching in the field fifty yards away. There was something odd about them but Vanessa didn't notice what until one of them patted the other on the helmet to give him the signal to fire.

114

"Oh shit!" Vanessa just about had time to say as a bright white flash raced towards her to block out the crack in the door. She dived behind a line of cages but she might as well have taken shelter behind a pack of eggs for all the good it did her. The shoulder-mounted RPG had been designed to take out tanks on the battlefield so it easily obliterated the Thatchers' rusty old corrugated chicken shed and everything inside with shrapnel to spare.

The explosion lit up the night and was seen by everyone, human and otherwise. To Larousse, the detonation looked like a glorious smite from God but to Bingham and 18 it looked like an act of desperation. The rockets had been brought to stop vehicles from fleeing, not barbecue poultry. This particular theatre of combat and this particular enemy needed a more ordered approach, not less.

"Hold your fire, Goddamnit!" Bingham barked into his radio as burning feathers rained down across his people from on high. "Rocket team pull back. And no Willy Peter either."

Henry and Angel couldn't have known about the change in orders though. As far as they were concerned the ante had just been upped and whilst sticks and stones might not have troubled their bones, Rocket Propelled Grenades were another matter altogether. They stayed crouched against the side of the barns until the fires dimmed enough for them to take advantage of the shadows again. If one positive had come out of the explosion it was that most of the soldiers had momentarily lost their night vision. Henry and Angel suffered no such ill effects and as such were able to slip past several formations before making it back to the farm.

The front door was too exposed but there was another way in, and it was the same way Mrs Thatcher had come out – down the coal chute. Henry jumped in feet first closely followed by Angel. They slid down the short drop and landed in a seemingly empty cellar but Henry wasn't taken in by the discarded ropes and the vacated chairs. He could smell Sebastian even if he couldn't see him, something that had less to do with Henry's superhuman abilities and more to do with Sebastian's scattergun approach to Paco Rabanne.

"You can come out if you like."

An upturned bucket appeared from behind the sofa and Sebastian lifted it off to ask: "Who's winning? Us or them?"

To Sebastian's surprise a second bucket popped up next to him, this one containing Mr Thatcher, who'd taken the opportunity and the liberal wearing of buckets to share Sebastian's coveted hiding place with him.

"Get away from me," Sebastian baulked, shoving Mr Thatcher and his bucket out of his personal space which, when it came to serial killers, was wider than usual.

"Anyone else down here, Sebastian? I mean, besides yourselves," Henry asked, his nose already working overtime to smell past Sebastian and Mr Thatcher.

"Well there's a few hop pickers in the fridge over there," Sebastian replied, pointing them in the direction of Mr Thatcher's mates in the corner.

"That weren't nothing to do with me, honest. That was the wife," Mr Thatcher maintained, trotting out the party line and insisting every problem could be traced back to Mrs Thatcher as if he were Ken Livingstone on coke.

Angel took a step towards Mr Thatcher and glared him into silence. He was a worthless stain on humanity as far as she was concerned. She killed because she had to, because she needed human blood in order to live, but the Thatchers had no such necessity. They killed because they liked the act killing. They might have butchered and eaten their poor unfortunate victims afterwards but that merely served to consecrate the joyous misdeeds. It had nothing to do with subsistence. They were sadist murderers, pure and simple, and their type had plagued mankind since before the first vampires had ever appeared.

"We pick our hosts very carefully," Angel told Sebastian, which was true. Every Coven meeting took place at such a charnel house. They were isolated by tradition and each resident maniac usually went to great lengths to keep their nosy neighbours at bay. Occasionally the Coven would let their hosts live, if the circumstances were mitigating enough, but more often than not they did everyone a favour and buried them out in their bone yards alongside their own victims. How many rueful runaways and trusting travellers they'd saved by observing this practice was anybody's guess but this wasn't the intention. The Coven didn't kill for philanthropic reasons. It simply made good commercial sense to cut down the competition if the chance arose.

"Yeah well, it's all worked out a treat, hasn't it?" Sebastian had to say several times to be heard above the rattle of machinegun fire, adding "No offence" when he Angel had turned to glare at him.

"Don't worry, we're not going to kill you," Angel reassured him.

"What about me?" Mr Thatcher asked hopefully.

"You belong in one of your own jars," Angel growled before relenting. "But then again, who are we to judge?"

The atmosphere eased a notch or two now that everyone had played their cards but Henry was still stressed. He felt the weight of his own immortality bearing down upon him and it wasn't something he was shouldering comfortably. Dying was never easy, but at least for most creatures it was inevitable and accepted as such. But Henry and Angel hadn't had to think about death (not their own, at least) for more than five hundred years, substantiating the old adage "the more you have, the more you have to lose".

"Don't worry, this isn't over yet," Henry told Angel. "We still have a chance."

Angel knew to what Henry was referring and gave him a supporting embrace. "If anyone can do this she can," Angel agreed.

CHAPTER 19

Across the courtyard, on the other side of the farm, Fourth Squad had taken up positions to defend a dirt track that snaked through a little gully and disappeared into the darkest part of the woods. If anything got past them they'd never see it again – until it was too late.

Forth Squad had yet to see much action yet but were prepared for anything. They'd seen what had happened to First Squad and they were determined not to have their names inscribed in the same piece of marble. As such they kept every weapon trained on all points leading to their carefully defended positions.

Just as the worst of the mayhem was dying down in other parts of the homestead, Sergeant Harefield heard a strange noise that grew louder and louder with every passing moment. His men heard it too and braced themselves for the inevitable onslaught but none of them could've predicted what was about to emerge from the shadows.

Thud thud thud! Thud thud thud! Thud thud thud!

"Steady lads, steady. Pick your targets and make your shots. Here we go," he said.

A suddenly movement caused eight muzzles to train on the same figure.

"Excuse me, but could somebody help me? I can't walk very fast," Alice said, thud thud thudding her zimmer frame steadily closer towards Fourth Squad.

Two of the Sergeant's men chuckled and lowered their weapons but the Sergeant barked at them to stand fast and get ready to fire.

"Oh no, don't do that. I'm not one of them, you see. They held me prisoner," Alice pleaded without success, fooling no one. The guns remained pointing at her and the Sergeant warned her to turn back. It was better she was kept in the farm until the sun came up than tangled with now.

Alice took exception to the young man's tone of voice and leaned into her walker with an undisguised contempt before

118

telling him, "If you let me through, I might even let one or two you live."

Despite the Sergeant's best efforts and Alice's warning, a giant of a man, known to friends and enemies alike as 23, stood up and withdrew 2ft long machete from its sheath.

"I got this one," he told his comrades.

"23, retake your position, that's an order," Sergeant Harefield shouted but 23 wasn't about to back down and be accused of running scared from a little old lady, undead or otherwise. He approached Alice with his machete drawn and poised to strike. The blade was so sharp that it could've felled a tree trunk as thick as 23's forearm in a single swipe. And with seven red dots lighting up the old lady's cardigan, the lads had his back if she sprang any surprises.

Alice quivered as 23 drew nearer. She'd had bunions for the past 900 years and they were really playing her up tonight (of all nights), bloody things.

23 stopped the other side of Alice's zimmer, knocked her hat off and grabbed her hair stop her from pulling her head away.

"Sorry my dear but this might smart a little," he chuckled, swinging his machete back a last few inches to maximise its swing.

Alice slapped 23 in the chest, knocking the wind out of his sails with her surprisingly sprightly strike, but not so much that it threatened to put him off his stride. But then 23 suddenly felt very queer indeed; a dizziness swamped him accompanied by a horrible nausea. The machete dropped from his hand and he felt himself sway. And then, just as he fell to his knees, he saw something wet and dripping in Alice's hand. It was his own beating heart.

"Some people never listen," Alice snapped, as 23 coiled over onto his face to die.

"Fire fire fire!" Sergeant Harefield shouted, lighting up the night with tracer fire as they raked Alice back and forth across the open dirt track.

But the old lady was like a blur. One second she was in one place, the next she was elsewhere. Before he could empty his cartridge, 30 looked up to see she'd closed thirty meters and was now bearing down on him. She snapped his neck and leapt at 28 before the former's gun had hit the dirt, still firing in futility long after Alice had swept through them.

Sergeant Harefield saw their bullets were having no effect on Alice. Unlike Chen, Alice had barely any muscle to stop their rounds with; consequently their bullets passed through her like a knitting needles through wool. The more they raked her the angrier she got. She must've still felt something but she didn't let it show. Now was not the time to dwell on her pain. Now was the time to serve it back tenfold.

Sergeant Harefield shifted his line of fire from her body to her head to at least disorientate her but the thought had occurred too late and she was suddenly on top of him, teeth glistening and nostrils flaring.

"No respect for your elders, that's the world's problem today," Alice snarled as she pulled the Sergeant's head from his shoulders and threw it at 34 to lay him out too. Only 33 remained, stumbling back and slinging his gun away as useless as he tried to flee.

Alice laughed. There was no getting away from her in this mood and 33's flight was only pressing her buttons all the more. She yanked him back before he got to the trees and held his face in her hands.

"Not running from old granny, are we?" she chuckled, her fangs engorged and her eyes blood red. "And after I knitted you a scarf as well."

She now pulled the tangled monstrosity she'd been knitting all week from her pocket and wrapped it around 33's neck. His eyes bulged and the veins popped out of his temples as he choked but Alice wasn't trying to strangle him, merely to build up the pressure in his arteries so that when she bit into his neck, the spray would saturate her senses in a way that she found almost orgasmic.

"There there," she smiled as he fought to claw her hands away. "Hush little bunny".

Alice now leaned in and licked his neck. No soap or aftershave. Just how she liked it. She was about to bite when a white-hot pain skewered her from behind.

She looked to see 34 lowering his crossbow and felt her chest to find an arrowhead poking through.

"Now that was uncalled for," Alice gasped as 34 reloaded but there was no need. He'd scored a bullseye first time. She was dead before she hit the ground. At least she would've been but she didn't make it that far. A sudden gust of wind came out of nowhere to carry her off on its breeze, leaving just her clothes and scarf for 33 to untangle himself from.

"What the fuck was that?" 34 gawped as he prodded her cardigan and overcoat only to find more ash.

"I don't know, but maybe the dementia tax isn't such a bad idea after all," 33 replied, feeling somewhat underpaid after all.

CHAPTER 20

The battle was over. The two sides withdrew to lick their wounds. And count their dead.

Some of the outer buildings were ablaze. Burning chickens and red-hot shot had ignited several hay bales and now the resident horses and pigs were kicking at the doors of their filthy paddocks and squealing in panic as the flames crept closer.

Colonel Bingham lowered his binoculars as his units radioed in their successes and failures.

"*Three of them bugged back to the farm, Colonel, but we neutralised the other,*" Third Squad reported in.

"*We nailed one on the western track,*" Fourth Squad, or what was left of them, echoed.

"And how many did we lose?" the Colonel asked.

When the counting was done the figure seemed to suggest nine all told.

"Dead or wounded?" Larousse demanded to know.

"There are no wounded, Mr Larousse," Bingham replied with contempt.

"We've barely two Squads left, Captain. That's not enough to hold this place," Larousse objected.

"They're down as well, Mr Larousse. There are only three of them now and they're hurt. They won't try that again."

Bingham turned away from his Larousse and headed up the hill to get on with the business of repositioning his pawns. There were still hours until dawn and his troops had been decimated and yet they were somehow hanging on.

"Actually sir, there are four of them," a voice called to him from behind.

Colonel Bingham turned to see three of his men traipsing up the hill with an offering that almost made this whole catastrophe worthwhile. Battered, burnt, bloodied and bruised, a woman stared back at Colonel Bingham with malicious eyes. She was tethered around the neck with strong wire and held at arms length between the two soldiers with snare poles while the third kept the crosshairs of his crossbow sights trained on at all times.

"Give that man a cigar!" the Colonel uttered, staring at Vanessa with a mixture of horror and greed.

Larousse was equally stunned and asked with incomprehension, "Is that one of them?" scarcely believing what he was seeing. Few men got this close to the Ungodly ones and those that did rarely lived to tell the tale. And yet here they were with a living, breathing demon in their midst.

"So, how's your night panning out?" Vanessa asked sardonically, almost as interested to meet Bingham as he was to her.

"What should we do with her, Colonel?" the soldier with the crossbow asked.

Colonel Bingham edged nearer – not that much nearer, just a little – for a closer look and marvelled at the unnatural forces at work in Vanessa. Her clothes were shredded and singed from the force of the RPG blast and yet her lily-white skin beneath was all but unblemished. Vanessa watched Bingham as he examined her and wondered if she should offer to drop her pants and bend over too.

"Magnificent," he said, so full of admiration that he almost wished he could switch sides – it wouldn't have been the first time he had – but ultimately the Colonel concluded it was too late in the day to defect now. Besides, it might mess up his plans to see out his remaining years counting his money and lying on a tropical beach, sipping cocktails.

"Please! We have to kill her now. She's too dangerous to hold," Larousse pleaded, breaking the spell Vanessa had cast over the Colonel.

"What, little old me?" Vanessa simpered, making a mental note of the chink in the Bingham's ranks.

Bingham nodded and the soldiers either side of her yanked on their respective poles to choke her by the throat. Vanessa reacted instinctively, snatching back at the poles and almost pulling the soldiers off their feet.

"Desist!" the soldier with the crossbow warned her and Vanessa reluctantly heeded his warning, if only to live long enough to see these fuckers skinned for their impertinence.

Colonel Bingham was impressed with the demonstration and smiled broadly. "I think I'm in love," he laughed.

"Then here, kiss me," Vanessa replied, puckering up as best she could to hide her engorged fangs.

"Sir?" the soldier repeated, eager for the order to kill her and neutralise the threat. But Bingham wasn't about to look a gift horse in the mouth and gave the order that made Larousse's toes curl in dread.

"Break out the frame."

CHAPTER 21

Boniface seemed to be back to where he'd started; in the Thatchers' kitchen and staring at the same tablecloth they'd all found themselves admiring earlier. Only this time he found himself alone.

Boniface liked his own company. He would've been a loner had he lived a normal life, so immortality suited his temperament. And yet there were times when companionship was desired – like now for example, when a merciless enemy had him surrounded on all sides and was intent on wiping him from the face of the Earth. He could've done with another friendly face just now but the others had all left him.

He wondered if any of them had made it. If they had, it was clear that none of them had doubled back and taken on the enemy from behind as agreed. The treacherous bastards! He knew he couldn't rely on his so-called friends when push came to shove.

Why had he even come here tonight? Indeed why did they even need a Coven or a European Council? Why couldn't they go their own way and do their own thing, as nature intended? The strong hunted the weak. They always had and they always would. What more was there to discuss? Snakes didn't have rules. Sharks didn't have rules. Lions didn't have rules. Or at least, they didn't have quotas. They had rules of another kind but they didn't vote on them. The biggest lion just roared and all the others went away and brought him back a zebra. Why couldn't they do that?

Naturally, it didn't occur to Boniface, not even for a moment, that he might not necessarily be the biggest lion.

A creak behind an internal door caused Boniface to jump. He grabbed a chair leg from amongst the rubble and braced himself for the final round of this evening.

The brass handle clicked a couple of times, the hinges groaned as the rickety door swung open and Boniface swung his weapon.

"Careful now. You're liable to hurt someone with that," Henry warned him with a smile, causing Boniface to check his swing at the last moment and breathe a sigh of relief.

"Fuck!" Boniface said, tossing his weapon away as his colleagues climbed up out from the cellar to resume their meeting. As relieved as he was to see Henry and Angel again, Boniface would've rather never seen either of them (or this place) again. Their gambit had failed, their numbers had dwindled and their hopes had faded as a result.

"Are we the only ones who made it back?" Boniface asked righting a chair and retaking his place at the conference table – or rather, the Duke's old place. And it didn't go unnoticed.

"Not quite," Angel replied, peeking out of the window to make sure the night held no more surprises – for now.

Sebastian trudged out of the cellar and acknowledged Boniface with a smile before finding his own chair to flop into.

"Perfect. My night's complete," Boniface sighed.

"You and me both, chuckles," Sebastian agreed, lighting up, this time without asking for permission.

Angel looked around the smashed up room. The place hadn't exactly been the Ritz before but now it looked more like the Blitz.

"Oh Lord, the missus is going to go nuts when she sees this lot," Mr Thatcher gasped when he emerged from the cellar to join the rest of the party.

"I think you're safe on that front," Henry reminded him, and Mr Thatcher's face fell when he remembered.

"Oh. Oh yeah," he nodded, his grief rekindled but his sense of purpose suddenly lost. He'd loved Mrs Thatcher, he truly had. And she'd loved him. They'd been soul mates and no two hearts had beaten more closely, particularly whilst pickling their postmen's privates. He set about straightening a few pictures on the walls but it would take more than a hoover before the old place looked back to its best. Not that much more but a little.

"So, what do we do now?" Angel asked in case anyone else had any bright ideas. She'd meant it for Henry or Boniface's consideration but it was Sebastian who ultimately answered, putting his brains into gear and asking himself what he would do in their position –*not* the vampires but the soldiers up on the hill.

"Why don't you try talking to them?" he suggested, puffing on his fag and scratching his head to show he could multi-task as well as come up with fantastic ideas.

"Talking to them?" Henry frowned.

"Yeah, you know, strike up a pow-wow. What have you got to lose?" Sebastian asked.

"They want to exterminate us," Angel pointed out.

"Yeah, well, they're probably saying the same thing over there about now, so why don't you go out and see what their best offer is? It can't hurt."

Henry wondered if Sebastian might have stumbled upon something. After all, this was what this whole evening had been about in the first place: talking; negotiating; resolving; the settling of differences through mutual agreement, albeit amongst themselves originally. Why not simply extend the conversation to the enemy outside? If nothing else, it might at least give them an insightinto their foe's resolve.

"So, how do we do that?" Henry asked, his negotiating skills a little ring rusty from five hundred years of simply taking whatever he wanted.

"You're not seriously asking him for advice are you?" Boniface objected vehemently.

"Hey hey hey, I know the score, mate. I've been around," Sebastian reassured the Coven with a little roll of the shoulders.

Boniface glared thunder at Sebastian as though he were being asked to explain his actions to an ant. "I'm over two thousand years old, boy. I fought at the Battle of Arbela. I followed Alexander through Asia. We conquered the known world and ruled as Gods."

Sebastian took this into consideration and then invited the ancient warrior to take a look at his current situation. "Yeah well, that's all well and good, shipmate but what have you done lately?"

Boniface was speechless. He had indeed trodden the known world, sacked cities, overthrown kings and taken the lives of thousands, both deserving and otherwise, but in all that time he'd never met anyone quite like Sebastian. How was it that this guy was even still alive? And Boniface didn't just mean tonight. In general terms. How had Sebastian not been murdered by someone already? It was almost inconceivable. He was exactly the sort of person who should've met with some grisly encounter long before now and yet here he was, in the presence of vampires, serial killers and a death squad outside, sticking his head into the AGA to light his withered cigarette whilst metaphorically flicking elastic bands at Boniface's testicles. It defied logic that he should've even been here in the first place and it was clear from the smirks on Henry and Angel's faces that they felt the same. But then, perhaps that was *why* Sebastian was still here. Because his continued being was so improbable that he'd crossed the threshold from unlikely to miraculous, summoning up St Jude, the Patron Saint of Lost Causes, to guide Sebastian to safety, just as he had done with the crew of *Apollo 13* and Leicester City Football Club a few years earlier.

A scream rang out in the night to break the tension. It was a female voice but not a human one. The scream was too powerful, too primal, too incensed. No mortal woman could've mustered that much hatred.

"Vanessa," Henry deduced. "She's still alive."

And so she was. High on the hill, and beneath a silvery moon, the Colonel's men tethered her by her hands and feet to a titanium A-frame that had been designed to hoist artillery pieces into place but was now struggling to contain Vanessa's fury. The Colonel oversaw the procedure and instructed his men to choke her every time she struggled, which was most of the time.

When she was finally secured to the frame, the relieved soldiers were able to safely withdraw their snare poles and beat a tactical retreat. Vanessa continued to protest her outrage at Bingham and Larousse but neither man moved. Bingham watched on impassively whilst Larousse itched to plunge his long hot stake between her ribs. In fact the feeling was so strong in him that it had almost taken on a sexual connotation, made all the more intense by Vanessa's helpless vulnerability. Vanessa could sense it. Colonel Bingham could sense it. An off-duty lighthouse man in John O'Groats could sense it. Larousse's intensions were transmitting so loud and clear that half the tellies in Sussex were currently being slapped.

"You're hurting me. Cut me down you bastards! Cut me down, you filthy scuttling roaches," Vanessa protested, gyrating this way and that against the ropes that held her fast. She had a great body and Larousse made free with his eyes, ogling the long rips in her clothing to take in her milky flat belly and curvaceous white thighs. How he would've loved her all to himself. His inner sadist could've found an exquisite release but the Colonel wasn't about to leave him alone with their golden goose – at least not until she'd feathered all of their nests.

"What's your name?" Bingham asked, taking a cautious step towards her.

"Death. And I'm coming for you," Vanessa replied, flashing Bingham her fangs to underline the point.

The Colonel caught her by surprise with a punch to the face that would've ordinarily felled an ox, but Vanessa shook it off with a flick of the head and resumed her glower.

"You should know better than to hit a lady?" she told him.

"You are no lady, my dear. I don't know what you are, but I do know how to kill you and this man will do just that you if you try anything," he said, ushering the soldier with the crossbow forward to stand guard over her.

The threat was clear and Vanessa reined in her fury. She would die tonight, of that she sure, but until her heart had actually been ripped in two, there was still a chance. There was always a chance. She hadn't lived for a thousand years without coming close on a few occasions so while her outlook was bleak her best hope was to play for time.

Larousse shadowed Bingham and edged nearer for a closer look but the Colonel told him in no uncertain terms: "If you touch so much as a hair on her head, lay a finger on her funny parts or harm her in any way at all, you will die. Do you understand that?"

"You don't know what you're doing," Larousse replied, reluctant to appear cowed in front of Vanessa.

"Maybe not. But there's a science team arriving at dawn who do and you know what I say; always best to leave these things to the professionals," the Colonel said, trudging back down the hill and to his forward position.

"And then what?" Larousse called after the Colonel.

"Then me and my men are retiring, somewhere far from here," the Colonel called back, adding as an afterthought; "and very fucking sunny."

When Bingham was gone Larousse turned back to Vanessa and continued his appraisal.

"Like what you see?" she whispered softly as he examined her more closely. "Because it could be yours, every night, and in every way conceivable way… for all eternity."

It was not an offer without its merits but Larousse was a man of God — and he reminded himself of that fact as much as he could as Vanessawrithed before him in the most alluringly wicked ways imaginable.

CHAPTER 22

18 kept his eyes on the farm. He'd barely taken them off it all night. As long as he knew where *they* were, he knew which way to run should he suddenly find the need. Fear lay in the unknown. Monsters of the imagination lurked in the darkest of shadows. Whilst on active service in Sierra Leone, 18 had seen some truly awful things but the thing that had disturbed him the most had been a huge great hairy black spider lollygagging on his cot. 18 had grabbed a bat to dispatch it with but in the blink of an eye it was gone. He'd torn his cot and his bivouac apart looking for it but never saw it again – except in his imagination… every time he closed his eyes and tried to get to sleep.

18 had no intention of losing sight of the monsters in the farm just as he had that spider. If he did, sleep would be all he'd ever know. And it would last for an eternity.

Colonel Bingham approached 18's position and dropped down beside him.

"Anything?"

"It looks like the other three erm… er…" 18 stuttered, unable to say the word out loud.

"It's okay, you can call them vampires if you like. No one'll laugh," Colonel Bingham reassured him.

"Oh, well the other three vampires are back in the farm with two warm bodies," 18 said, rechecking the thermal image detector to make sure they were still where they were meant to be. Sure enough two red silhouettes appeared on the screen standing in what was left of the kitchen while the odd ripple of heat shimmied to and forth between them to suggest they were alone.

"Probably the vampires' clothing," 18 explained, "catching a few degrees of heat each time they pass in front of the AGA."

Colonel Bingham reached for the thermal image detector to look for himself. "Who are the two warm bodies? Ours?"

"Negative sir, I'm guessing it's the farmer and that other one: the one they brought with them."

"Why haven't they killed them?" Colonel Bingham pondered out loud, watching the red silhouettes pacing the room freely like lion tamers inside circus cage.

"Perhaps they're keeping their options open," 18 hedged a guess. "It's what I'd do."

Colonel Bingham liked 18's thinking. It was outside-the-box logic. After all here they were, three inhuman monsters, whose sole purpose in life, according to Larousse, was the exportation of death, and yet they were happily tolerating, nay even allying themselves with their prey in the face of an even greater threat outside. This suggested some sort of tactical thinking, which meant the creatures inside were no mere inhuman monsters but an enemy in the truest sense. Firepower and strength would not be enough to defeat them. It would also require brains.

"So tell me 18, what will their next move be? What would you do?" Colonel Bingham asked. A second opinion always helped, particularly from an out-of-the-box thinker like 18.

"If it was me, sir?" 18 said, thinking on the predicament for a moment or two before concluding; "I'd make a deal."

*

Less keen on deals or truces with the enemy was the pious Larousse.

The vampires were right where he wanted them, trapped inside a house with guns on all sides and the dawn fast approaching. All he now required of them was their screams as they roasted alive before him. Tomorrow promised to bring about a glorious rebirth for Larousse. It should've been something to rejoice but the Colonel's treachery had threatened to spoil his buzz. Larousse had to make him see the folly of his ways. These creatures were not to be underestimated. And there was only one way to do that – with information.

"How many of you are there?" Larousse asked Vanessa, pacing backwards and forwards as she hung spread-eagled against the A-frame before him.

"Enough to farm you like cattle if we wanted to," Vanessa cackled in reply.

"Then why don't you?" Larousse asked, stopping to stare at her.

"We prefer our meat free-range too," she replied, adding for mischief; "as God intended."

Larousse duly bit and flared his nostrils in indignation. "What do you know of God?" he scowled.

"More than you I'd wager," Vanessa teased him with a wink.

Larousse flushed scarlet but reluctantly concluded she was probably right. If this foul temptress was indeed an envoy of Satan, then she would've known more about God than he, just as someone playing for Arsenal would've been more familiar with the boys at Spurs than even the most ardent Spurs fan would. Vanessa was an insider playing the greatest game of all, that of good versus evil, while the Larousse was on the sidelines, an outsider who'd simply picked a team to support.

Until now.

"How old are you?" he asked, getting back to his interrogator's script.

"Now you're just getting personal," Vanessa pouted coyly, stoking Larousse's secret fires as well as his curiosity.

Larousse picked up his bag of tricks and pulled something out.

"What is that?" a voice beside him asked.

"Just a light," he assured his crossbow-toting sentry. "May I?"

The sentry was reluctant to give permission without the Colonel's express say so but then again he was equally reluctant to refuse the man who, up until an hour ago, had been paying him. He decided to take the middle road and simply reply with his feet, turning around to look the other way.

The small neon tube was obviously more than "just a light". It could emit different wavelengths – infrared, ultraviolet, X-ray and gamma etc – to reveal an object's true appearance under different frequencies. Larousse had tested in on certain types of butterflies to reveal the full spectrum of their wing displays (before pulling them off obviously) but this would be the first time he'd used it on *one of them*.

He turned the light to infrared and ran it up and down Vanessa's body to confirm she was ice cold, no heat pattern whatsoever. Now he switched the neon tube to Ultra High Frequency and tried again.

"My God," he said, when he saw the results.

Where up until now the woman before him had appeared young and almost airbrushed, the light revealed an altogether different picture. Between the tears in her clothing her body looked ravaged by the sands of time. Black veins and a leathery skin reflected back against the orange hue. Larousse traced the light over her withered breasts, across her desiccated throat and up towards her demonic face. Vanessa grinned like a medieval gargoyle at the horrified look on Larousse's face.

"You should see me in daylight darling. It's even less flattering," she told him.

"Oh I plan to," he replied dourly. "Make no mistake about that. When the Colonel's got what he needs from you, you will *see the light*."

Vanessa laughed. Her gambit had paid off. She'd reeled him in and now, without him realising it, he was standing within striking distance of her. Quick as a flash she struck out against the ropes, lunging at his hand and sinking her fangs into his knuckles.

Larousse yelped in pain and tried to snatch his hand away but Vanessa hung on for dear life, sucking on his juices and crunching bone until his arm ran with blood.

His and hers.

Larousse finally fell to the floor and clutched at his gnawed knuckles, howling in pain and about to call a medic when a terrible thought occurred to him. Vanessa confirmed his worst fears when she looked down and laughed; "Now we can enjoy it together, darling".

Larousse's blood turned to ice. Yet this was no mere shock but a permanent state of affairs. His temperature was plunging as his nature life ended. Now he was through the looking glass. Now he was off the sidelines and into the game for real.

"Colonel Bingham!" the sentry called, shifting the aim of his crossbow onto Larousse. "Colonel, we've got a situation here!"

This couldn't be happening. Not now. Not to Larousse. There had to be a mistake.

"Wait, no, please!" he pleaded, but like Vanessa's pleas only minutes earlier, his words found deaf ears and merciless hearts.

CHAPTER 23

Down in the farm, the vampires were unaware of the latest and most surprising addition to their Coven. They were far too busy arguing amongst themselves over how to save their asses — their souls were beyond redemption. As ever, when confronted with a clash of ideals, they had reverted to what they knew and put Sebastian's proposal to the vote.

Boniface stood in the middle of the room, his hand aloft, and looked around at the others in resentment.

"Okay, one," counted Henry, just to make things official. "And who says we go with Sebastian's plan?"

Four hands shot up as Boniface put down his but he objected to one of them and snatched at Mr Thatcher's hand. "He doesn't get a vote," he snapped cantankerously.

Even with Mr Thatcher's ballot disqualified it was still a landslide by any margin so Henry turned to Sebastian and gave him the floor.

"Okay, it's decided. So, what's your big idea?" he asked, eager to hear what tricks Sebastian had up his sleeve. It was a complicated strategy but luckily Sebastian had a way simplifying it so that even he (as in himself) could understand it.

"Well, have you ever seen a film called *Zulu*?" he asked.

Four stony expressions stared back at him to tell him he might need to elaborate. Mr Thatcher vaguely remembered the movie and thought it starred Michael Caine and Stanley Baxter whereas Angel remembered the public's reaction to the actual battle, having picked off one or two tasty morsels who'd toasted the Royal Engineer's eleven Victoria Crosses a little too heartedly on the home front.

And yet neither of them could see what relevance it held for them now.

*

As a military tactician, Colonel Bingham could've probably helped shed some light on Sebastian's idea but unfortunately for him he had other things on his mind, namely a second A-frame to break out and assemble to accommodate his latest prisoner.

"No no no, please don't do it. I am God's envoy, appointed by the Synod and ordained by the Bishop of Rome himself," Larousse was howling as they shackled him to the frame. He was considerably easier to restrain than Vanessa had been. His strength had yet to materialise while his shock had yet to abate. He was putty in their hands; a compliant rag doll and the Colonel took particular pleasure in exacting as much terror from him as he was able to. Unlike Larousse, Bingham wasn't a sadist by nature, but there were of course exceptions and this was one of them.

"I hope the irony's not lost on you, Mr Larousse," Colonel Bingham smiled as he pulled Larousse's wrists above his head with a yank of the ropes.

"Please Colonel, please, set me free, I implore you. I'll do anything for you. Anything you want. I don't want to die," Larousse began blubbering, almost pricking the Colonel's sympathies – almost, but not quite.

"Be grateful it's me still in charge. There are some around here who would see you burn in the morrow's sunlight," he reminded him, only too happy to expose Larousse's puritanical streak for the evil it was.

Vanessa chuckled with delight as Larousse wailed in despair.

"You have your subject now, Colonel. Why not let bygones be bygone and set me free?" she proposed.

Bingham stared at her in the moonlight. She was indeed a magnificent creature. He had no personal grudge against her but he couldn't let her go. Not if he wanted to walk away from this place tonight with his throat intact. What was the expression? *When you sup with the devil bring a long spoon.* As such the Colonel was reluctant to leave the table until his spoon stretched across several time zones.

And skewered his dinner dates to their chairs.

18 shook his thermal image detector. One of the hot bodies in the farm below had disappeared from the screen but 18 couldn't understand how.

"Where the hell did he go?" he asked himself, convinced it must be his equipment rather than his vigilance. But he looked again and sure enough, only one red silhouette remained in the farmhouse. The other had seemingly dropped off the face of the Earth.

The radio crackled in 18's ear to answer his question.

"*Sir, we've got movement,*" 33 radioed in from the other side of the farm.

"What's happening?" Bingham demanded.

"*You'd better come for yourself and see. I think… I think they want to talk,*" 33 told him.

*

Henry stood in open ground beneath a silvery grey sky. The night was no longer pitch black. The darkness was beginning to drain away. It was almost imperceptible to normal eyes but Henry was only too aware of the change. The hourglass was emptying. And their sands were slipping away.

Colonel Bingham took a few minutes to circumnavigate the farm to where Henry was waiting. He studied him through his binoculars before he got too close and concluded he did indeed appear to want to talk. He looked unarmed except for a white flag and a human hostage who was kneeling beside him with a flour sack over his head. This cleared up the mystery of where the other warm body had gone but not what Henry wanted. And there was only one way to find that out.

Colonel Bingham rose from the grassy knoll behind which he was crouching and stepped out into the open. Three of his troops went with him, two wielding crossbows, the other an SMG. The vampire might be prepared to walk out under a white flag without a weapon but the Colonel most certainly was not. A war zone was no place to be caught without a gun, white flag or otherwise.

Colonel Bingham approached to within twenty feet of Henry and his men fanned out behind him, their fingers at the ready should negotiations grow too heated.

Henry noted the Colonel's pips. He didn't belong to any army Henry recognised, which suggested a private force, which in turn suggested a limited number of resources. Sebastian's idea perhaps wasn't such a bad one after all and Henry already had a better idea of who he was facing before either man had even opened their mouths. He yanked Sebastian's jacket collar to warn the soldiers not to come any closer and was rewarded by an understanding nod from the Colonel and a muffled outburst from beneath the flour sack.

"Good evening," Henry eventually said, figuring he should get the ball rolling as he'd been the one to request this meeting.

"Good evening," Colonel Bingham replied with a raised eyebrow. It always hearted him to find courtesy in the most unlikely of places and he was happy to reciprocate.

"How are you doing out here? It's cold tonight," Henry sympathised despite not being able to feel it himself.

"We're holding our own, thank you. And how about yourselves?" the Colonel said, noting he could see his own frozen breath as he spoke but none from Henry.

"We've seen better nights," Henry confirmed.

Colonel Bingham almost laughed. "I should imagine you have. A great many of them, I'd wager. You want to talk?"

"We want to go," Henry said, cutting to the chase.

"Go?" Bingham shrugged. "Go where?"

"Go home. Go abroad. Go anywhere this is not happening," Henry said. It was a request more than a demand and Bingham could sympathise. Henry and his cohorts hadn't come here for this fight and they weren't ready for it. But Bingham and his men had. And this gave them the edge, both tactically and psychologically.

That said Bingham was in no more of a mood to do deals with this devil than the one he had lashed up on the mound. But he continued to the dialogue anyway. Just out of courtesy.

"Why should we let you go?" he asked. It was a reasonable question and deserved a reasonable answer. Fortunately Henry had one pre-prepared.

"Have you ever seen *Zulu*?" he asked.

In his youth Bingham had been a great fan of war movies. Not too many mercenaries got into the business off the back of Disney cartoons, so of course he had seen *Zulu*. It was a classic. A small band of British soldiers, hopelessly outnumbered at Rorke's Drift, and destined for immortality. Although, in their case, not literally. But Bingham could see the parallels.

"I've seen it," he confirmed.

"Good. That should speed things along," Henry said to himself.

Bingham pre-empted the conversation and tried to outline what Henry was suggesting in non-Michael Caine terms. "You're proposing an honourable withdrawal? One set all and let's leave the field with a mutual respect for one another?"

That sounded good to Henry. "Something like that?"

"How very civilised," Colonel Bingham smiled.

"Enough have died tonight – on both sides. And neither of us wants that to continue."

Bingham glanced at the men on either side of him. None of them flickered. None of them flinched. He had their loyalty and their belief. They would follow him to their ends of the Earth. But who would've guessed they would find it in Sussex.

"I agree," Colonel Bingham conceded. "But we are trapped here just the same as you. You might be inside and we might be outside but neither of us can leave. As well you know."

"Look around you," Henry urged his opponent. "You've killed more of us tonight than any man has in a thousand years. Your place in history is assured. Go and get your rewards. We're ready to let bygones by bygones – if you let us go."

Bingham regarded the creature opposite him. He looked like any normal man: average height, average weight, average build and average looks. He would've blended into a crowd of two and been gone before you knew it. This thought unsettled Bingham more than anything he'd seen tonight and he didn't much fancy the idea of ending up like 18 and unable to go to sleep without turning over his bed first.

"Supposing we did just let you go? How would we know that you wouldn't turn around and kill us the moment you got out?" Colonel Bingham asked, setting out his concerns with an understated smile.

"Because there's something else we want," Henry told him. "Our friend you're holding up on the hill. We'll trade you: one of ours for one of yours." The flour sack once more erupted with a tirade of obscenities and objections, much of which was fortunately censored by a sock in the mouth.

Colonel Bingham glanced at his watch and noted the time. Dawn would be here soon enough. At which point they could decamp their positions in the forest and move in. Incendiaries and petrol would do the difficult job for them and they could knock down the roof and sifted the rubble at leisure until they were satisfied that everything and everyone inside could pass through a cook's colander. Then, and only then, would Colonel Bingham relax.

"What's your name?" Bingham asked Henry.

"Does it matter?"

"I guess not," Bingham conceded. "Do you know what I have at the moment?"

"Tell me," Henry said.

"Certainty. And for that, uncertainty is no exchange."

And with that, Bingham drew his sidearm and shot both men before him. The soldier with the SMG lent his support, peppering Henry and Sebastian with short bursts while reinforcements rushed forward at this given signal to lasso Henry around the neck with snare poles.

"Snag him. Get his arms. Get his neck," Bingham directed his men until Henry was caught, just as Vanessa had been earlier.

"You bastard! You bastard! You could've walk away from this!" Henry screamed. "You could've lived!"

"If only I could say the same about you," Colonel Bingham replied, waving Henry's white flag in front of him before tossing it across Sebastian's dead body at their feet.

*

It took four of them with snares pole to drag Henry across the fields and up the hill towards the next hastily erected A-frame but Colonel Bingham was determined to take him alive – at least for the moment.

He had quite a little collection going.

"You can still walk away from this. You can still live!" Henry berated the soldiers as they strung him up against the frame with wire ties.

"Make them tight," Colonel Bingham told his men. "Don't worry, he's tough, he can take it," he added, giving Henry a little wink.

It took all of their strength to restrain Henry and all of their guile to avoid his teeth and claws but after ten minutes of struggling Bingham's men were finally able to step back and admire their handiwork.

"You bastards!" Vanessa screamed at them all from the adjacent A-frame. "You bastards. You'll pay for this you will. Your whole families will pay for this."

"And put a muzzle on that one," Colonel Bingham directed. Vanessa was duly gagged but Larousse was left to jabber in terror for the Colonel's amusement.

"Yea, though I walk through the valley of the shadow of death, I will fear no evil: For thou art with me; Thy rod and thy staff, they comfort me…"

It sounded to most of the lads nearby like the 23rd Psalm but unfortunately for Larousse, he was well beyond deliverance, either from above or below, and he knew it. His blood had frozen solid in his veins and his senses had spun off in all directions. His transformation was all but complete but it would do him no good. He was a newly hatched butterfly falling from his cocoon and straight into a spider's web. The sun would boil his body and the devil would take his soul. Nothing would be left of the late Mr Larousse but a sense of sadistic satisfaction in the pit of the Colonel's belly.

Henry glanced across at his newest comrade and knew whatever happened he wouldn't make the grade. If Boniface had blackballed Sebastian, Larousse would have no chance of joining the Coven.

"Last chance, Colonel; release us or die," Henry warned the Colonel as he hung suspended by the wrists a few feet from the smiling soldier.

"And disappoint my benefactors?" Bingham shrugged dismissively.

"Whatever they're paying you, we can double it. Money is no object to us," Henry said, still trying to reason with the man who was planning on selling them to medical research.

142

"As tempting as that might be, I'm afraid I am a man of my principles. And they bribed me first," Bingham replied.

This ignited a fury within Larousse that surfaced in a misplaced tirade of righteousness. "The Synod will not rest until they find you. You have betrayed all that is sacred. You are no better than they are."

Bingham laughed. Not least of all because Larousse was still referring to the vampires as "them" and "they" when he should've been saying "us" and "we".

"The Synod took twenty years to find these assholes, Padre. And that was only once they hired me. I think we'll take our chances. What do you say boys?"

Bingham's men laughed in agreement. At least most of them did. 18 was a harder nut to crack. As a veteran of the 2003 invasion of Iraq, he remembered George W. Bush's speech delivered two months later on the deck of the USS *Abraham Lincoln* in which he declared, "Mission Accomplished". Up until that moment, British forces had suffered 33 casualties, only to lose a further 146 men in the weeks and years after George's speech before finally pulling out in 2011. American losses were even greater. George W. Bush himself 'somehow' managed to escape the war unharmed.

"I'm going to do something I haven't done in over six hundred years," Henry told Bingham sternly.

"Oh yes? And what would that be?" Bingham asked, allowing Henry his say.

"I'm going to enjoy killing you," he snarled.

Bingham smiled. "I like your confidence. If only we could bottle that too."

CHAPTER 24

Troopers 40 and 41 were returning to their reserve positions after helping capture Henry when 40 signalled to 41 to stop.

"Wait!" he said, sweeping the track with his infrared headgear when he saw something in the trees ahead.

"What is it?" 41 said, readying his gun in case anything sprang out at them.

The night was black and still, almost unnaturally so. There wasn't even a breeze to stir 40's breath and yet he could've sworn he saw a few leaves flickering against a backdrop of deathly calm.

"It's nothing," he concluded once he was satisfied the track was clear. "Just thought I saw something."

But 41 didn't answer. He couldn't, because 41 was no longer there. 40 turned at the lack of a reply and saw only empty space at his shoulder. The night had swallowed 41 up without a trace.

"What the hell...?" he just had time to say before he too was sucked into the shadows and spat out without a sound.

Two less bolts in Bingham's ring of steel.

*

The first hint that something was awry was the sudden burst of radio traffic in Colonel Bingham's ear. As the officer in charge he kept track of his men's communiqués whether they concerned him or not. Now they most certainly did.

"*40? 41! Are you there, over? Come in please 41. Check in, over!*"

Colonel Bingham listened for either 40 or 41's reply but neither gave one. Nor ever would again.

"*41? Can you hear me, over?*" the radio asked again.

No reply.

"*42, have 40 or 41 checked in with you yet, over?*"

Nothing.

"*42, are you there, over?*"

Silence.

"*For Christ's sake will someone please reply, over?*"

Dead air.

"Colonel, I think we have a problem, over."

A sudden scream in the night caught everyone unaware and an accompanying burst of gunfire further away endorsed Bingham's fears.

"What's going on, over? Anyone and everyone. Report in immediately," Bingham demanded, taking charge of the situation.

"There's something out here, sir. There's something in the woods," the reply came back as more gunfire and screaming echoed in the distance.

Bingham looked up to see pinpricks of muzzle flashes in the foliage towards the east. That was beyond their lines. Something was happening to their rear.

"That's impossible," Bingham barked into the radio. "All of our targets are contained."

"Negative sir, it's out here. It's all around..."

But Colonel Bingham was left to fill in the blank for himself because the transmission was cut dead and only static remained.

"Soldier, come in. Soldier? Report in, Goddamnit!"

But no one was left to report in. Section three was gone.

"You had your chance," a voice called out. Colonel Bingham turned and saw Henry glaring back knowingly.

*

Once breached, Bingham's lines began to crumble quickly. No one knew which way to look or, indeed, for what. Foxholes were abandoned and positions deserted as the panic set in.

A black shape streaked across the woods drawing gunfire from all quarters but nothing seemed to stop it. 33 had lost 34 in the woods as they retreated back to the trucks but they wouldn't get far. Something grabbed 33's collar and swung him with immense force into the trunk of a tree to knock the wind from him.

He squeezed the trigger but shot only air as his head was yanked to one side and he found himself staring into the eyes of his own death.

"Too little, too late," Boniface told him as he ripped his throat out with a swipe of his claws.

33 sprayed him with rivulets of warm blood but Boniface didn't care. His suit was back at the farm, carefully folded and placed over a chair. These were Sebastian's clothes he was wearing.

See, whilst all eyes had been on Henry throughout his tete-a-tete with the Colonel, no one had thought to look under his hostage's flour sack. Everyone had naturally assumed it was Sebastian because he'd worn Sebastian's clothes. He'd even had a trace of heat about him thanks to his clothes being placed on the AGA first. But the whole meeting had been a subterfuge: a sleight of hand to get Boniface into the shadows. Henry knew they weren't about to talk their way out of here. But if he could get outside, beyond the farm, and close to the trees, he might just be able to draw their attention while 'Sebastian' (aka. Boniface) rose from the dead and slipped away unnoticed.

Now Boniface was clear, in the woods and at the back of their persecutors, as per their original plan.

But unlike Colonel Bingham, he had no intention of taking prisoners.

*

More shots and more screaming rang out in the night but this time from a different direction. Boniface had cleared a gap in the lines and Angel had slipped through to join the fun.

Unlike Boniface Angel enjoyed killing for sport. She liked it very much in fact. For her, hunting soldiers on the hoof was as good as it got and she dashed this way and that, picking them off with a snap of the jaws like a terrier snatching at rats.

34 felt something at his back before he heard or saw it but all at once his face was in the mud and something heavy was on his back.

"Wait…!" he yelped but Angel bit his pleas in two as she clamped her teeth around his larynx.

His racing heart just fed her faster and once drained, she leapt off him and into the trees, disappearing as fast as she had appeared, to leave 34 facedown in his own sludge.

*

Like Bingham, 18 knew the game was up, but unlike the Colonel he had an exit strategy he'd been working since they'd started decorating the place with vampires. He reasoned, quite logically, that if the enemy had slipped through their lines and were now attacking them from the rear, the one place they wouldn't want to linger would be the farm, the place in which they'd been pinned down in all night.

He scanned the buildings with his thermal image detector one last time and saw nothing down there but the AGA. The two hot bodies had now both disappeared and the cold bodies were never there to begin with.

"Fuck this!" he said when a new batch of gunfire broke out to his rear. All eyes turned towards the source of the commotion and now 18 saw his chance. He slung the heavy thermal image detector into the nettles, glad to be rid of it, picked up an SMG and slipped away as his comrades began firing wildly in all directions in the gloom.

*

The reason 18 had been unable to find either warm body on his thermal image detector was simple: Mr Thatcher had fled the scene while Sebastian had been packed in ice. Unlike the rest of the occupants in the Mr Thatcher's freezer though, Sebastian was still just about within his Best Before date. Henry guessed the enemy had some kind of heat detector and needed to hide Sebastian's hot body if Boniface's Trojan Horse routine was to work. It would've seemed needlessly ungracious to have killed him – and that wouldn't have hidden his heat pattern anyway – so Angel suggested the freezer, stripping him off and bundling into the icebox alongside Mr Thatcher's crispy pancakes and Mrs Thatcher's tubs of Ben and Jerry's.

Although Ben and Jerry's what, Sebastian daren't look.

The lid of the deep freeze popped open at the second time of asking and Sebastian sat up with a creak. He was so blue he could've probably passed himself off as a Smurf had he had a white hat handy.

"F-f-f-f-f-f-f…" he tried to say, unable to swear and scarcely able to move.

His arms wouldn't work so he used his legs to hoist himself over the side and onto the stone floor below. He landed with a thump and cursed the Thatchers for not having an upright freezer in which to store their victims.

A wood burner stood smoking across the cellar so Sebastian wobbled to his feet and staggered over to it like Boris Karloff climbing off the laboratory slab.

"F-f-f-f-f-f-f-f…" he continued to attempt, hunkering over the wood burner until his teeth stopped chattering. It took a while for the sensation to return to his arms and legs but when it did he almost wished it hadn't, they ached so much.

"F-f-f-f-f-f-f-fiddlesticks!" he finally got out, pleased to be able to speak again if not actually swear. That would come back with time.

Sebastian lit a fag and took and long loving drag before looking around for his clothes. Damn, he remembered now, Boniface had taken them all and a right knob he'd looked too. Some people just didn't have that crucial 'it' factor to make such high-end threads look cool. Sebastian did but Boniface, and obviously the bloke who'd given them to Oxfam Shop in the first place, didn't.

Sebastian needed something to wear. It was cold outside and he couldn't hitchhike all the way back to London in his pants – not without ending up in someone else's freezer. Luckily, sitting there neatly folded and awaiting their rightful owner's return, was a suit and tie combo that had come through this whole scrape almost unscathed but for a dash of plaster and a drop of blood.

Sebastian donned Boniface's clothes without a second's thought. Fair exchange was no robbery, he told himself.

*

Henry and Vanessa could see the panic in the soldiers' eyes. Something was coming for them and it was coming for them fast. Death and desperation stalked the night and nothing could stop it. Gunfire and flashbangs tried in vain to slow its pace but the screams just kept getting closer until a deathly silence fell across the whole forest.

For the few soldiers left guarding the prisoners, that seemed more terrifying than anything else.

"What do we do, sir? What do we do?" a soldier holding a crossbow on Vanessa asked.

Bingham was conflicted. He'd got what he'd come for in the shape of three live prisoners, only to lose them at the eleventh hour. Damn it, where was that science team?

Another scream called out in the night, this one barely a stone's throw away. Bingham was out of options. And when Henry started shouting "Over here! We're over here!" he knew the gig was up.

Vanessa tried joining in but her gag was too tight. Larousse on the other hand had no such restraints and with the prospect of deliverance so close, he cast God to the wind and threw his lot in with the Devil.

"Help me. Please help me. I'm one of you now," he cried, making up Bingham's mind once and for all. Dying would be bad enough tonight. But knowing that he'd died and Larousse had lived would torture him for all eternity.

"Kill them. Do it quick," he instructed his men, picking up Larousse's own stake from where he'd dropped it and pressing the point to his chest.

"No, please Colonel. Don't do it. You don't have to do it!" Larousse desperately pleaded, out of his mind with terror.

Bingham smiled as he fixed him eye-to-eye.

"I know I don't, Mr Larousse. I just want to," he told him, driving the stake as hard as he could until Larousse's accursed black blood spurted out of his mouth.

"Damn you...!" Larousse whispered as his body crumpled and his hands snapped off at the wrist. He hit the dirt but barely made a thud; his uniform contained nothing more than dust and the charred stain of a burnt-out soul.

Colonel Bingham hadn't expected that to happen and clearly neither had his men. They stood around gawping at Larousse's empty battle fatigues and looking at each other in shock before the Colonel reminded them they had two more prisoners to execute.

"You son of a bitch!" Henry seethed as Bingham picked up Larousse's stake to use once again and the crossbow-wielding soldier took up aim opposite Vanessa.

149

Now she was done for. Now she was dead. It wasn't a case of lost hope but of seeing the soldier's finger squeezing the trigger and knowing that the agonising pain that was about to follow would be the last thing she would ever know.

But Vanessa had one last card up her sleeve. It was a card of last resort and few vampires ever played it because it didn't delay their deaths, it merely reclaimed ownership of it.

Henry knew what she was about to do but he couldn't stop her. And before the bolt had left the crossbow Vanessa welled up with the force of almighty hell and unleashed it upon herself, obliterating her body and knocking her would-be murderer for six with the force of the blast.

Bingham found himself on the ground and wondering how he'd ended up there. He looked up at Vanessa and saw she was gone, only a cloud of red mist hung around the A-frame she'd been tethered to while the soldiers who'd tried to kill her was lying some ten feet away with a crossbow bolt sticking into his own neck.

But this had been more than about simply taking her killer with her. Henry still had a chance. And with her sacrifice, Vanessa had bought her oldest and closest friend a few more precious seconds.

CHAPTER 25

27 was in the clear. He'd abandoned his post and left his mates for dead but it was a decision he could live with. He was a soldier of fortune, not misfortune. Some people died for their friends but not 27. He preferred his friends to die for him.

Like Bingham he'd served in no regular army. He'd got into this game after escaping the Scrubs and had headed south to avoid the authorities, stopping only once he found himself in Chad.

It was here that he'd first held a gun and it was in Benin that he found he could turn it to a profit. Half a dozen wars later and he was a veteran with a reputation if not a name, at least not in the UK, not anymore.

27 stopped in a little gully and listened. He was in the deepest darkest part of the forest, waist deep in bracken and surrounded by pines. He could still hear gunfire and screaming in the distance and reckoned himself to have made at least half a mile. The farm and the main road lay southeast. He would head due west, through the densest woods and the roughest terrain. It was his own particular tactic. When the shit hit the fan and the dead started piling up, don't bolt for the quickest escape route, head cross-country. It was the surest way to leave friends and foe alike far behind.

27 could see the sky starting to glow above the forest canopy. The dawn was fast approaching. He'd take to open ground once the sun came out but for now he would stick to the trees. It felt like the safest option.

He squinted through the shadows one last time then decided to keep moving, making for a gap in the bracken at the crest of the next hill. He never made it. Something popped up out of the ferns to block his path. It was too close to shoot and too quick to avoid. A blow to the neck knocked 27 down and suddenly something was straddling his chest.

"Trespass on my land, will you! Frighten my chickens, indeed!" Mr Thatcher raged as he pounded 27's head with his meat cleaver. 27 didn't stand a chance; he was dead before Mr

151

Thatcher struck the fourth blow but that didn't seem to faze Mr Thatcher who just went on chopping, over and over again until his cleaver hit mud and 27's head rolled away down the hill.

"You won't get away from me like that," Mr Thatcher barked angrily but then stopped when he sensed someone was standing just behind him.

He turned his head slowly and saw Angel leaning against a tree watching him with delight, her eyes glowing red in the darkness as though they were smouldering.

"He was like this when I got here," Mr Thatcher assured her. "I just found him like this."

"Oh really?" Angel replied, pushing herself off the tree.

"It wasn't me, honest. It must've been the wife."

And with that, Mr Thatcher quickly rolled off 27, grabbing his SMG and squeezing the triggering to empty the clip in Angel's direction.

He was fast, very very fast.

But unfortunately for him, not fast enough.

*

18 was likewise running for his life, through the farm, across the fields and into the trees on the other side of the valley. Death and destruction had rolled through here already and 18 stumbled across the evidence, tripping over one former colleague and sliding on what was left of another. There was very little left of either of them. Throats were gone, as were hearts and in some cases, limbs, but 18 knew better than to sit around conducting autopsies on his mates. They were dead. And he knew what had killed them: the same thing that would kill him if it got a hold of him.

18 jumped to his feet and motored on, leaping through the brush and going for broke in the direction of the main road. If he could just get to concrete there were few men nor beasts who could run him down over open ground. Not when he had the Devil at his back.

"One, two, three, four," 18 counted off, just as Bingham had instructed him to do the last time he found himself fleeing through the woods. This time however, he failed to get to five.

"F… ooofphhh!" he groaned, running bang smack into something without seeing was it was. A gangly figure had come crashing out of nowhere and ploughed straight into him, knocking him for six and sending him and his SMG spinning off into the undergrowth. But 18's training quickly took over and within a second he was back on his feet and ready to fight. He might've lost his gun but his will-to-live was fully loaded and he was ready to get messy if need be. He pulled out his combat knife and slashed the air between them as he sized up the opposition.

His attacker stood up, turned and stared at 18. 18's eyes narrowed. His attacker's eyes narrowed. 18 crouched in readiness to strike. His attacker reached out for a log. 18 circled one way. His attacker circled the other.

Neither dared move.

Then, without warning, his attacker tossed his log aside again.

"Hold on, hold on. Time out," he said, holding out his hands to show 18 he was packing nothing more than short arms and yellow fingers.

18 stared at the figure opposite. He looked like the human who'd tried fleeing the farm at the start of this evening, only now he was wearing one of the vampire's clothes. Who the fuck was this guy that he could get the shirt from a vampire's back?

"Look, we don't have to do this," Sebastian said with a hush, looking from side to side to make sure no one else was eavesdropping.

"What?" 18 gawped, not sure he understood him right.

"Let's just pretend we didn't see each other, yeah? No one needs to know," Sebastian suggested, nodding in agreement at his own plan.

18 thought on this for a moment or two. He was a professional soldier, hired to do a job. He had the training, the ability and the experience. He even had the weapon. He could've carved up this civilian in an instant. On the other hand, so many people had died already tonight, many of them needlessly, what difference would one more or less make? And if this guy could

153

survive a house full of vampires then perhaps it wasn't his time to die anyway.

18 thought on the dilemma then made up his mind. He chose life over death, both for himself and the charmed young man opposite.

"Sounds good to me," he said, sheathing his knife and continuing on his way.

Sebastian watched him go with a sign of relief, up the track and into the long shadows until he could see him no more.

"Mind how you go now mate," he said to himself, looking to the heavens and thanking 'whomever' for blessing his fellow traveller with that most precious of gifts – the gift of reason.

CHAPTER 26

But while peace had broken out on the cut-through to Christ's Hospital, the war was still raging back up on the hill.

Colonel Bingham regained his senses after Vanessa's self-destruction and armoured himself with an extra layer of kevlar. He only had Henry to go but he wasn't about to end up like his trooper with a loose bolt sticking through his jugular. No, if Henry wanted to blow himself up, Colonel Bingham would ensure it was a controlled explosion.

He hovered the stake over Henry's heart and braced himself for any funny business.

"It's a bit old school, I know, but it should still do the trick," he assured Henry with a smile, slamming the stake into his chest only to find it barely sunk in an inch. He tried again and met with the same results before realising that Henry had donned his own set of kevlar, only tucking it in beneath his shirt.

"That won't stop me," Colonel Bingham promised him, using his combat knife to cut away at Henry's layers until he reached skin and bone.

"You're mad," Henry told Bingham as he grabbed the wooden stake again. "You're throwing away the chance to have something that Kings have tried to trade their Kingdoms for."

"Kingdoms are overrated," Bingham replied. "I value my privacy."

Bingham saw Henry's eyes glance to the left but he was too slow to respond. A burst of automatic gunfire cut through the pair of them, knocking Bingham to the ground and finishing off Henry's jeans once and for all.

Bingham tried to reach for his sidearm but it was plucked from his hand and tossed into the bushes to join the rest of Bingham's spent forces. A tall figure squatted over him as he squirmed in the mud and bared his fangs at Bingham.

"You killed a lot of my friends today," Boniface snarled, breaking out into a smile and giving Bingham a little wink. "Thanks."

"Enough trumpeting. You want to cut me down or what?" Henry called over to Boniface, eager to get his own hands on Bingham, and scratch his own backside, but not necessarily in that order.

Boniface took the stake lying neck to Bingham and approached Henry on the A-frame.

"So, I get the Duke's old territory, do I?" Boniface said, picking up negotiations where they'd left off earlier that evening, only from a more advantageous barging position.

Henry was dumbstruck. "I don't believe this. You're really doing this? Really? Really?"

"Yeah really?" Boniface confirmed. He'd had enough of Scotland. He'd been there for about eight hundred years now and was ready to use the stake on himself. Eight hundred Scottish winters could do that to a man. This was the chance of a lifetime – nay a hundred lifetimes – and he wasn't about to let it slide.

Henry recognised a winning argument when he was confronted with one and conceded the point.

"Fine, take it. It's yours if it makes you happy."

"That does. That makes me happy," Boniface concluded, cutting the ties that held Henry's wrists and looking forward to his new life in the Smoke. He'd not seen London since 1236. He wondered if it had changed much. "Good meeting," he said, freeing Henry of the last of his bonds and helping him to his feet.

As grating as it was to see Boniface come away from this get-together with everything he could've hoped for, it was a relief to be free again and Henry celebrated his release with a flexing of his fangs.

The next thing he did was pick up Bingham's blood trail and follow it down the hill to where the Colonel was attempting to flee. He hadn't got far. About ten feet in all but it was the thought that counted.

Henry rolled him onto his back, indifferent to the pain it caused him and stared into his eyes just as they'd done earlier, only this time with the tables turned.

"Just so you know, we would've kept our word. We would've let you and your men leave if you'd let us go," Henry

156

said, only too aware that this knowledge would torture Bingham more than any red hot poker possibly could.

"Bullshit. You're a monster. You know only death," Bingham gasped, trying to roll over as he coughed on his own blood.

"There was only one monster here tonight. And it wasn't I," Henry disagreed.

Bingham had nothing to add to this. It was all immaterial now anyway. He'd come to the end of the road and there were no alternate endings for him. He lifted his head to expose his neck and told Henry to get on with it.

But Henry wasn't about to let Bingham off that easily.

"You should've taken our offer," he scowled, his teeth engorged and his eyes blood red as he fulfilled one of his vows at least – and claimed his first human victim in six hundred years.

CHAPTER 27

Sebastian tripped over his own feet and managed to sustain his stumble until he'd found something cold and hard to plant his face into. As it turned out it was a road. He looked left and then right and remembered it as the one that led up to the entrance of Thatcher's farm. He'd made it out! Somehow he'd got away.

Nothing moved on the road in either direction, including Sebastian, so he jumped to his feet and started chasing down white lines until they took him around a bend.

Sebastian stopped. There, parked on the hard shoulder, was an army truck. The lights were off and no one seemed to be at home but Sebastian took it one step at a time. He hadn't come this far just to run into a bayonet now. He peered into the cab and saw that it was empty. He did the same in the rear and clocked only ammo crates and wanking socks. The truck was his for the taking if only he could get it started. Of course he might look a bit conspicuous driving up Balham High Street in it but it would do for the first fifty miles just to get him out of here, so he climbed in and ran his hands around the cab feeling keys. Whoever had parked here was obviously a fan of tradition because he'd left them in the sun visor and Sebastian caught them as they attempted to flee.

"Back of the net," he smiled.

Sebastian had never driven a truck before but he was willing to give it a go. After all, trucks were only big cars with more wheels and no rear view mirrors but he wasn't planning on reversing anyway so what did it matter?

He twisted the keys in the ignition and woke the engine up with a roar. It sounded powerful. It sounded fast. And it sounded very fucking noisy. He stuck the truck into first and started pulling out onto the road.

THUD!

Sebastian had barely gone two feet and he'd hit something already, but what? He couldn't see anything out there. There was no other traffic, he was clear of the trees and he was steering away from the fence.

A pair of legs stepped down from the roof off the cab and onto the bonnet and Angel crouched down to smile in through the windscreen.

"Going somewhere?" she asked with a smile.

Sebastian was played-out. He'd got so close to getting away only to be pegged back on the home stretch. He was no longer fearful, just exasperated.

"Oh come on, let us go, will you? After all we've been through," he sobbed, feeling like a condemned prisoner who'd received a Royal Pardon on the morning of his execution only to discover it was invalidated because of poor punctuation.

Angel swung through the passenger window to take the seat next to him. Against the glare of the dashboard dials he could see her mouth and chin glistening with something wet that wasn't sweat. She wiped her face with a sock she found in the footwell and threw it out of the window.

"We need a ride," she told him.

"You've got cars, ain't you? You came in cars," Sebastian reminded her.

"The sun's coming up," Angel said, pointing to the orange hue in the east. "We can't drive in daylight."

Sebastian drummed his fingers against the steering wheel and thought on the predicament. At least they needed him for something. As inconvenient as this was, it was preferable to not being needed at all. He still had a few cards to play yet.

"Then will you let me go?" he asked.

"Of course Sebastian," Angel reassured him. "We're nothing if not appreciative."

Sebastian restarted the truck and drove back towards the farm. They stopped at the gates and waited. Both he and Angel were reluctant to go any further and they stared at the old Thatcher's place from a distance. It looked even grimmer in the early dawn's light. The house was swathed in shadows and masked with mist. The outer barns had burnt to the ground to leave nothing but ashes and old girders twisted in a smoking heap while the hillside was littered with dead. Had he really only arrivedhere eight hours earlier? It seemed like a lot longer.

"Are you a betting man, Sebastian?" Angel asked.

"I like a flutter from time to time," he admitted, wondering what she was proposing he put up as a stake.

"Then I'll bet you £10 that you never read about any of this in tomorrow's newspaper."

Sebastian wondered why this might be. Was it because dead men read no newspapers or was she hinting at something more sinister? Sebastian chose to play dumb. It was a tactic that had got him this far while all the smart guys were sleeping out there in the mud so why change now?

"I might need to go to a cashpoint," he said hopefully, only to have his hopes dashed by a distant scream.

Sebastian reached for the ignition but Angel steadied his hand.

"Relax," she told him. "Just some friends of ours."

A moment later they saw movement in the trees. Two figures stepped out and started towards them. Even from this distance they could see that one was Henry and the other was Boniface, albeit wearing Sebastian's clothes.

Angel jumped down when they reached the truck.

"You made it," she said, giving Henry a relieved embrace.

"Just about," he shrugged then looked up into the cab. "Hey Sebastian, thanks for sticking around."

"No problem, you know me," he tried to smile.

It was then that Boniface noticed Sebastian was wearing his suit. It had taken him a moment because it no longer looked like his suit; it was battered and torn, muddy and soaked. It was going to require the dry cleaning equivalent of Victor Frankenstein to save it from being cut into tea towels now.

"You want to swap back?" Sebastian explained when he saw Boniface gawping.

Boniface growled but was sanguine. "Keep it," he replied. "Something to remember me by."

"Vanessa?" Angel asked more in hope than expectation.

Henry shook his head sadly. "We're all that's left."

Angel looked to Sebastian and suggested: "You can still change your mind and stay with us if you like. Can't he?"

"We have had a few vacancies crop up of late," Henry admitted, putting it mildly. "Mr Boniface?"

When this same question had been put to him at the start of the evening, Boniface could only object. And it wasn't because of what had happened with Thomas or because of who Sebastian was, it was simply because he hadn't been consulted beforehand. Boniface was a man of immense pride. But looking around the smoking ruins on Thatcher's farm and the valley of death it sat in, Boniface was ready to concede that satisfaction had been done. Honour had been restored – to him, at least.

"Up to him," he shrugged as disinterestedly as he could. "I withdraw my objection."

Sebastian didn't know whether to laugh, cry or attempt to run them all down in his truck, but he tried to look pleased all the same, if only for their benefit. They might have been mindless killers but they were curiously touchy with it.

"So Sebastian, how about it? Ready to join the family?" Henry offered with a smile.

As tempting as it was, eternal life, superhuman powers, nice teeth, there was a downside too. And that wasn't just meeting up with Boniface once a century. There was the nocturnal existence, religious persecution and eternal damnation to take into consideration, not to mention his holiday to Corfu that he'd already paid the deposit on.

"Can I think about it?" Sebastian asked.

"Think about it while you drive," Henry told him, climbing into the back with Boniface and Angel and pulling the canvas flaps down to keep the rising sun out.

Sebastian started up the engine and turned the truck around. The open road beckoned but not all roads led to Rome and someone had nicked the Satnav.

"Where to?" Sebastian asked.

Henry's called through from the back and echoed Sebastian's own thoughts. "Anywhere but here, Sebastian. Anywhere but here."

Sebastian couldn't have agreed more and gunned the accelerator to leave Thatcher's farm far far behind. It was only once they rejoined the main road a thought occurred to him.

"Here, what about my bag?"

EPILOGUE

The farm lay still in dawn's early light. The only things to move were the smoke drifting across the fields and the fox scampering between the ruins, now free to fill his belly with as much barbecued chicken as he liked. Nothing else stirred.

The shadows got shorter and the mists burnt away. It had been an eventful night for the fox but for someone used to running from buckshot and dodging dogs it was not entirely without precedent. Death and desperation went with the territory when you were a fox. But the object of the game was to ensure it always landed at someone else's door.

The fox's ears twitched. He could hear something approaching in the distance: more cars and heavy trucks, but it wasn't the same truck that had left an hour ago.

The fox decided to quit while he was ahead and slunk back into the woods taking one last fried chicken with him. He wasn't hungry but it was free and only going to waste. And who didn't love a takeaway at the end of a long evening?

Two bright white cars and one impossibly clean lorry stopped at the entrance of the farm. They could be seen for miles and looked conspicuous amongst all the mud and mayhem.

The occupants of the cars climbed out and surveyed the scene before them. Like their cars the clothes they wore were spotlessly white and package fresh. How could anything be so clean in this pit of hell?

The truck honked its horn several times and attempted to make contact via its radio but all efforts failed. The fox had already fled and there was no one left alive to hear it.

The back of the truck rolled up and several men in bio-chemical suits jumped out. They spoke with the person in charge, an immaculately dressed young woman of indeterminate age. Like everyone else she was dressed entirely in white but she had an air of power about her. In a different setting you might've taken her for a businesswoman or a lawyer or a politician or a powerbroker but here, in amongst all the death and destruction and blood and bones, she looked more like a concentration camp

162

commandant, which was probably the closest comparison to the truth.

She dispatched the men in bio-chemical suits and watched as they headed into the contamination zone. Six men dispersed in six different directions, some towards the barns, some into the house, some into the woods and a couple up to the top of the hill.

The sun continued to climb, shooting brilliant yellow rays through the skeletal branches of the trees to reveal more bodies scattered around the grounds.

After several minutes the woman in white's radio burst to life.

"You'd better get up here, Ma'am. It looks like we've got a live one."

The convoy drove into the grounds and parked beside the farm but they didn't head inside. Instead the woman in white and her entourage climbed the hill towards the rise, passing what was left of several soldiers and a very disappointed-looking Mr Thatcher along the way. His eyes stared straight up into the sky, unseeing and unblinking, the image of Angel etched into his corneas for all eternity. He'd lived a violent life and he'd died a violent death. It might've seemed a fitting end for him but there was more to his story than that. He hadn't always been a killer. In fact he'd been a very happy child until that fateful night in 1986 when he'd stumbled upon Melissa, roaming naked in the woods, looking for…

But what did that matter now?

He was dead and so was she. And after the woman in white was finished with this place no one would ever see or hear from them again. It would be as though they'd never existed at all.

"This way," a voice called out as the woman in white made her way up to the crest of the hill. Here she found three A-frames, two of which were empty but for rags and dust. But the third, the frame in the middle, contained the figure of man who could've passed for 200 years old. His face was crinkled and cracked, grey and grizzled, desiccated and decrepit. She could tell by his uniform that he was a soldier. And she could tell by his

163

pips that he was an officer. But she couldn't tell anything else from looking at him. Not even if he was alive. Not until he spoke.

"You took your time, you fucking bitch!" he hissed, his cracked lips parting to reveal a fearsome set of pearly whites, a parting gift from Henry and Boniface.

"Colonel," the woman commanded, snapping her fingers in his face to get his full attention, "where are the others?"

"Gone," he croaked, every effort causing him exquisite new agonies. He felt as though he was on fire, but not ablaze. Not yet. The sun had yet to make it over the crest of the rise so Bingham had been left to roast over a slow flame. And he was nearly done. "Get me down and I'll share what I've got with you," he told them. "I'll share it with you all."

But it wasn't exactly the most enticing offer in the world. Bingham was literally crumbling to dust before their very eyes. His lips split as he spoke and several teeth fell away but with little or no signs of blood. Just agony and ash accompanied Bingham's disintegration.

"Quickly," the woman said, summoning an assistant forward who held a silver briefcase. The case was opened and the woman in white removed a syringe from a Styrofoam surround.

"Cut me down!" Bingham ordered, but the woman was no longer listening. She had but a few seconds left to save her sample so she plunged the syringe into Bingham's neck and stirred it around as she looked for a vein, untroubled by her subject's screams. Liquid blood began to squirt into the syringe so she drew back to plunger to purloin as much as she could while the Colonel hollered in fury.

Her sample retrieved, she yanked out the needle and handed it back to her assistant who placed it into the briefcase and closed it to shield it from the sun. On the lid of the case a logo curled around some letters that read: "*Jeunes* by Infinity".

"Now cut me down. You've got what you came for so set me free," Bingham demanded but this time the woman didn't reply. She merely stepped back a safe distance and cocked her head, curious to observe what happened next.

The rest of the white-suited brigade joined her on the hill but no one went to Bingham's aid as his charred skin began to crackle.

"You have no idea how this feels. It's so incredible. I'll share it with you all, just cut me down!" he gasped as the first few rays of sun streaked across the hillside, over the trees and onto his back, casting his shadow across the woman in white.

Bingham screamed. He'd never known an agony like it and yet still the power that surged through his body was intoxicating. If he'd not been restrained he could've run up sheer mountains, smashed through walls, stalked anything that moved and swam through rivers of blood. His appetite was matched only by his ferocity and yet it wasn't a savage rage. His mind now functioned on a higher state of consciousness. He no longer identified with the beings opposite. In fact it was hard to believe he'd ever regarded himself as one of them. He was so much more in every possible way – a higher species even.

A fox amongst chickens.

"It's so powerful. So beautiful," he cried out as he burst into flames before them.

The woman in white barely batted an eyelash. No one did. And as Colonel Bingham burned to nothing in the first light of dawn, his screams brought to a close the 59th meeting of the 13th Coven of Nightwalkers (British Chapter).

Until the next time.

PRODUCTION NOTES

STORY ORIGIN

I first wrote *Eat Local* back in September 2005. Back then, and for most of the next eleven years, it was called *Reign of Blood*, a title it never suited and one I simply cobbled together out of several random scary words. *Blood*? Something *Blood*? Vampires like blood so it should probably have *Blood* in the title? *House of Blood*? *Night of Blood*? *Son of Blood*? *Reign of Blood*? That'll do.

Director Jason Flemyng came up with *Eat Local*. I didn't like it at first. Vampires suck, they don't eat. But it has since grown on me and I can honestly say that it fits the film, certainly more so than *Reign of Blood*, or as we came to know and abbreviate it, *ROB*.

Up until this point I'd only written a couple of screenplays. A meandering unfilmable version of *Milo's Marauders* and a straight-from-the-book adaptation of *The Hitman Diaries*, neither of which set the film industry abuzz. But they were helpful learning experiences nonetheless. They were my practice efforts and I was improving all the time, mostly how to structure screenplays and how to write without resorting to endless voiceovers to narrate what we were seeing onscreen. I'm not Mozart. This stuff doesn't come naturally to me. I wish it did but the truth is most of my writing is the product of years of trial and error, mostly error.

Back in 2005, *The Hitman Diaries* was optioned by an actor/producer called Martin Malone. Martin was sadly unsuccessful in his efforts to get the film made but I learned a lot from him, not least of all the restrictions a budget can place upon a film. Martin told me that more and more micro-budget films were being made because they offered less of a risk to investors.

This made perfect sense and yet bizarrely it had never occurred to me. I'd simply worried about story and dialogue and set pieces and explosions and left paying for it to someone else. But Martin was right. A film that could be shot for (eg.) £100,000 could be a more attractive proposition for a potential producer than a movie that cost £10million. Particularly from a first-timer like myself. So, taking a blank piece of paper and my new-found expertise in production budgets I sat down and tried to think of a scenario that might be shot cheaply. Or at least not prohibitively expensively.

Moving between multiple locations is apparently a very expensive exercise and time consuming. As is shooting in or around the general public (how much did a couple of scenes in central London cost the makers of *28 Days Later*? I don't know but I bet these few iconic scenes added up to a fair old chunk of the budget). So a single location, somewhere isolated and away from Joe Wave-At-The-Camera Public would make sense. Somewhere the crew could get in, set up their equipment and film the whole thing without having to pack everything away and move somewhere else.

A deserted farmhouse for example.

This is the reason deserted farmhouses and deep dark woods are so abundant in horror films. Not because they're scary. But because they're cheap. Horror films are generally made on lower budgets and deserted farmhouses and deep dark woods offer the producers the chance to keep their budgets down (eg. *Night of the Living Dead, Friday the 13th, The Evil Dead* and *The Blair Witch Project*, etc). In all honesty, you're probably a lot safer in a deserted farmhouse or the deep dark woods than you are on most city street but thanks to the straight-to-video industry we've come to associate these places with horror and death.

But who could I put in this deserted farmhouse and what could they be doing?

Serial killers don't really do it for me (too unpleasant), Zombies had been done to death and werewolves had recently run amok in *Dog Soldiers* but what about vampires? I liked vampires. They were my fiends of choice but a bunch of humans taking shelter inside an old deserted farmhouse while vampires stalked the woods outside was hardly an original concept. Incidentally, if you want to read a brilliant book along these lines, the best of its kind is *I Am Legend* by Richard Matheson. There have been three official film adaptations of it so far starring Vincent Price, Charlton Heston and Will Smith (the Vincent Price version is the closest to the book) but none of them are a patch on Matheson's original novel.

Also, as with my books, I generally find 'baddies' a lot more fun to write about than 'goodies' so it occurred to me to flip the premise and have the vampires taking shelter in the farmhouse while being besieged by humans outside.

From this starting point the story came together pretty quickly.

DEVELOPMENT

The first draft of the screenplay is fairly different from the film. For a start there were ten vampires not eight, there was no Colonel Bingham, just Larousse, and Sebastian was (believe it or not) the first to die, having already been turned into a vampire by Vanessa against strict Coven rules.

The script was more serious too, less comical, but it laid the basic foundations of what would become *Eat Local* about 30 drafts later (I stopped counting around the twelfth draft).

The biggest turning point in the development of *Eat Local* came when I met Jason Flemyng and Dexter Fletcher back in 2006. Jason and Dexter had optioned the rights to *The Bank*

Robber Diaries a year earlier but I'd not actually met them. I asked my [then] agent to set up a meeting or pass on a message to the boys but unfortunately setting up meetings and passing on messages, indeed like getting me book deals or replying to my emails, were talents far beyond my agent's limited skill sets.

Fortunately, luck intervened and Jason just happened to wander past the pub I was sitting in one lunchtime in Brewer Street, Soho, so I jumped up and ran down the road chasing him and his wife Elly through the streets of Soho. When I eventually caught up with them, it took me about another five minutes to get my breath back long enough to tell them who I was, as the 60 yard dash is not my strongest discipline, but Jason was very understanding and came back to the Duke of Argyll for a pint. We chatted and met up with Dexter a week later and kept in touch while they were trying to get the film version of *The Bank Robber Diaries* off the ground but unfortunately it wasn't to be. Most production companies felt it was too close to *Lock Stock and Two Smoking Barrels* to explore and eventually they had to give up the project as a dead duck.

It was then that I mentioned I had another screenplay, a low budget vampire screenplay, and so Dexter sent it to a few producers he knew. In his own words, "All the doors that had stayed shut to us while we were hawking *Bank Robber* around suddenly flew open". Why? Probably because *ROB* was obviously so much more doable on a limited budget than a sprawling bank robbery adventure that took the audience all over London. I hadn't started with a story, I'd started with a production concept and cut my cloth accordingly.

MARV (Matthew Vaughn's company) were initially interested but the script needed work. Jason, Dexter and I met up and tossed ideasaround, then I went away and worked on the screenplay. Colonel Bingham was born, Sebastian was allowed to live and Mr & Mrs Thatcher became serial killers. It became more or less the story that became *Eat Local* except that there were still ten vampires and not eight and would be for most of the next decade.

After a couple more drafts we had a fun and exciting screenplay on our hands that could be shot for around £1million.

MARV passed.

FALSE START

Dexter and Jason continued to try to get the film made over the next few years and several producers were attached, a couple of whom I never got to meet. One of these producers took *ROB* to the Berlin Film Festival where an offer of €250,000 was made to buy the rights. Unfortunately the screenplay wasn't his to sell, he was simply there trying to raise the finances to take it into production so the offer was never relayed to me. I only heard about this four years later (from someone who wasn't there either but who'd heard about secondhand) but it was too late to do anything about it. I don't know if it's actually true or not. People have been known to tell porkies in the film industry from time to time. Either way, it left me feeling like I'd washed and tumble dried a winning lottery ticket in my jeans pocket but what can you do? As we used to say on the building sites, you can't miss what you never had.

During this period Dexter and I got talking about an idea Dexter had been carrying around for 20+ years himself. It involved a dad coming out of prison to find his son fending for himself on a tough council estate and we worked the idea into the story that would eventually become *Wild Bill*.

Next to *ROB*, *Wild Bill* practically happened overnight. I finished the first draft in February 2010 and the cameras were rolling on it by the end of November. Incredible. The film turned out to be great as well and surpassed all our expectations, launching Dexter as a director and saving me when my book career hit the rocks.

It also led to a renewed interest in *ROB*, this time by *Wild Bill*'s producer, Sam Tromans, with Jason Flemyng directing. She had budgeted the film at £2million+ had investors lined up but on the first day of pre-production the money never arrived. The investors changed their minds and the project collapsed. This was through no fault of Sam and she tried again but was dashed a second time in quick succession. It looked like *ROB* was destined never to be made.

EVOLUTION FILMS

In November 2014 Rod Smith of Evolution Films dropped me a line. He asked if anyone held the rights to *ROB* and at that time no one did. He optioned it on the spot and said he was going to make it. I'd heard it all before but I signed the film over to him anyway as he bought me posh fish & chips to seal the deal.

Rod had previously worked as the Director of Acquisitions at Anchor Bay Entertainment. He'd been in the bidding for *Wild Bill* two years earlier and had been a fan of my writing so when he left to set up his own production company he made ROB his first target, with Jason directing. He didn't have £2million+ to produce the film (then again neither did anyone else) but he did have a healthy working budget regardless. In real money! Not promised money or projected money or bullshit money. Proper serious "I'm not joking" actual money. I know everyone thinks the film industry is awash with millions because actors like Daniel Craig and Kate Beckinsale can command seven-figure salaries but there's actually a lot less cash up for grabs than you'd think – probably because Dan and Kate have it all.

Nevertheless, we had enough to make the film and this time Jason and I were determined to do whatever we could to get it made.

The first thing we had to do was give the script a haircut. We had decent budget but in order to give Rod the biggest bang for his bucks we had to make several painful cuts, the first of which was reducing the number of vampires from ten to eight. It might not seem like much of a cut but there are a lot of people behind the scenes who need to be there in order to put those actors on screen, with make-up, costumes, prosthetics, cinematography, sound, transport, accommodation and food etc so that a simple cut and fold helped us get the best out of our eight remaining vampires. Believe me, if Sidney Lumet had been working with our limited resources he would've made *9 Angry Men* not 12.

Another snip involved losing a couple of big set pieces, a spectacular motorbike crash and a scene in a greenhousein which 18 is stalked through a hydroponics lab and only saved when he throws a switch and roasts his vampire attacker beneath a bank of UV lamps. Maybe we'll save it for the sequel.

Rod brought in GFM Films and Hereford Films to co-produce and in January 2016, a little over ten years since I'd first written it, *ROB* finally went into production under the title *Eat Local*.

CASTING

I had nothing to do with casting. Jason offered to involve me but I didn't want to do it again. I'd done it before with the BBC on my sitcom *Thieves Like Us* and it's not something I'd like to do again. Why? For starters, every struggling actor you've ever met contacts you out of the blue to ask you for a part. Of course they do, and who can blame them? But that doesn't mean they're any good or right for the role and if you fill up your film with drinking buddies just because you don't want to upset anyone you end up with something so bad that no one wants to go and see it except the people who are in it.

Also, I like to think of myself as a nice guy (it's a minority view) so when a desperate actor or actress is sat opposite me trying in vain to breathe life into my lines just so they can put the lights on back home, I genuinely want to help them. I don't get the power trip that some people get when interviewing applicants and ultimately you have to disappoint 99% of the people you see. It weighs on you, it really does.

That said, it was a sheer unadulterated joy to deny some of the nimrods who auditioned for *Thieves Like Us* gainful employment, one of whom was a stand-up comedian who didn't read from my script because he'd prepared his own material, telling me that he not only wanted to star in the show but write it too. Interesting tactic? Telling the person who's auditioning you that you're not only after the job on offer but theirs as well. He got neither. But such narcissists were few and far between. On the whole most of the actors and actresses who auditioned for *Thieves* were decent people who were simply trying to catch a break in an industry that boasts more jobbing bar staff than Wetherspoon's.

But still, back to *Eat Local*.

Lucinda Syson was in charge of casting but many of the parts were offered to friends of Jason. I know what I said earlier about not casting your mates but Jason has been around for many years and appeared in over 100 movies so his mates are of a better calibre than mine.

Charlie Cox (Henry), Tony Curran (Boniface), Robert Portal (Bingham), Johnny Palmiero (18), Jordan Long (Thomas) and, of course, Dexter Fletcher (Mr Thatcher) had all been earmarked their respective roles long before the film went into production, all of them glad to help out Jason as he directed his first feature film. This might not seem like much of a hardship to a layman, starring in a vampire action movie for a mate along with a load of other well-known faces off the telly. Indeed, as someone with one foot firmly planted outside the film industry and one toe tentatively in, I can appreciate that. But when someone like Charlie Cox flies in from New York fresh from filming the second series of *Daredevil*, or Tony Curran flies in from LA straight off the back of *Defiance*, to stand around in the cold dark woods at 3am for what amounts to little more than their expenses and a bacon butty, then it is a big deal, particularly when their profiles help lift the film's.

Freema Agyeman (Angel) was another who flew in from the States, having just filmed *Sense8* and *North v South* and there was no one more enthusiastic on the whole of the film set. She almost gave Jason a run for his money in terms of eagerness and there was nothing she wouldn't do to help out. In fact if we hadn't bundled her in her car when her scenes were done and

174

sent her packing we would've no doubt found her scraping the ice off everyone's windscreens at the end of every night. Come to think of it, I think I did see her at the lights down the road with a bucket of water and squeegee but fortunately the lights were green and I was able to put my foot down.

The part of Vanessa originally went to Mini Driver, who Jason had appeared with in *I Give It A Year*. Unfortunately, at the eleventh hour, she was unable to do it but we had a blinding bit of good fortune catching Eva Myles between jobs and she was perfect. In fact if you could've plucked the character of Vanessa out of my head and put her on screen, Eve Myles is exactly what you would've seen. What a trouper too, working an extra day on Sunday in a force nine gale and sleet storm just to get her scenes done and even I couldn't be arsed to do that. I was at home next to a radiator.

Mackenzie Crook (Larousse) was a complete surprise to me. I hadn't expected that bit of casting but he was just great and a perfect barometer for just how cold it was. In fact if you watch the first scenes in which he's talking to Bingham his jaw no longer works because it was 2am and -8°C and we'd all been in the woods for five hours already. Well, when I say we… it is a writer's prerogative to go home when it gets too cold. It's in the Writers' Guild handbook. Top fella though and very nice. Incidentally, Larousse got his name courtesy of my *Larousse Pocket Factfinder*. If in doubt your bookshelf is a great place to find your characters' names. If it's good enough for Ian Fleming,it's good enough for me.

I was particularly excited about the casting of Annette Crosbie as Alice. I was such a fan of *One Foot In The Grave* but obviously I couldn't tell her this when we met because I was playing it cool so I just stood quietly in the corner mouthing over and over again under my breath "Ooooohhhhhh Victor!" I like to think that Annette chose to do our film because in a career spanning more than 55 years she couldn't have been asked to fire too many M60 machine guns straight into the camera.

Ruth Jones (Mrs Thatcher) was another coup. Elly Fairman had been able to get a script to her via a mutual friend and she agreed to do it after liking what she'd read. That's a great compliment when someone of Ruth's stature signs on because she likes what I've written, not least of all because I had genuinely written it especially for her. Jason phoned me a week earlier to tell me he had a crack at Ruth and asked if I could write some Ruth Jones type lines. I did and she bit. So in a way the part of Mrs Thatcher was tailored for Ruth, as indeed was the part of Mr Thatcher. Dexter joined us for a couple of days just as he was getting ready for the premiere of *Eddie The Eagle*. He's a big-shot director these days so again we were lucky to have him, but he was great and stole every scene he was in, along with some tea bags and pencils from Labrokes earlier in the day.

Vincent Regan (The Duke) was another eleventh hour signing. We needed someone with genuine gravitas and authority to play The Duke but Charles Dance had already played three vampires in December and Christopher Biggins was in still tied up doing *Jack and The Beanstalk* in Nottingham. Fortunately Vince came onto our radar and he liked the character. It's funny, he's not in the film for very long but he has such a presence that you feel him long after he's departed. He looks like my cousin as well, but more he's a lot more fun to be around. Vince that is.

Lukaz Leong (Chen) is a stuntman and martial artist who appeared in Star Wars and 24, as well as zombie thriller, *The Girl With All The Gifts*. Jason was very keen on him playing the part of Chen and what he could bring to it, not least of all his death scene, which was much enlarged after Lukaz signed on. In fact, Jason's *Lock Stock* co-star, Jason Statham, came on board especially to choreograph and direct Chen's fight scene with the second unit, more about which later.

Finally the key role of Sebastian needed to be filled. Jason and Lucinda saw a great many up-and-coming young actors and while lots were good, none were quite right, not until they auditioned Billy Cook. Billy had a way about him that felt right. Sebastian might've had a posh name but he is anything but posh. There's a lad like Sebastian in every boozer and betting shop from Camber Sands to Carlisle: an ordinary lad of ordinary stock who likes a drink and a flutter and who would've found himself in a trench up to his knees in mud and still playing cards had he been born 100 years earlier. As the son of a famous pop star

(David Essex), Billy might not have been born on a rough and tough council estate but the mindset was clearly etched into his DNA. In fact, Sebastian was even given a Romani backstory after Billy Cook was cast because of his own gypsy ancestry, his grandmother having been a traveller and descended from Romanies. It was a piece of precision casting and I was happy for Billy too, as he was a lovely lad and very popular with all the cast and crew

Finally, there were a few notable cameos designed to help us pad out *Eat Local*'s IMdB trivia page, the first of which was Nick Moran (Private Rose). He is only in one scene. Indeed he was only on set for about an hour but his involvement marks the first time he, Jason Flemyng, Jason Statham and Dexter Fletcher have worked together since *Lock, Stock and Two Smoking Barrels*. Indeed a fifth *Lock Stock* star, Nicholas Rowe, also made a blink-and-you'll-miss-him cameo as Private Gary, who we see being dragged through the undergrowth and killed by Boniface in the final act. Again, it was done simply a favour from a friend and he came along to Putney Common one evening and got into uniform just so that we could drag him through some brambles four or five times before he went out for the evening. If he plays his cards right it could prove a big break from him.

Lastly, and most definitely leastly, I have an even briefer cameo as Private Woodcock, whose key role it is in Colonel Bingham's army to sit in a camp chair next to a field radio and try not to shiver. You can see me in a short scene over Mackenzie Crook's shoulder twiddling knobs and squinting up at the camera because I don't have my glasses on. In a longer version of the scene I even exchange a look with Mackenzie Crook but whether or not I pulled it off I couldn't tell you because I couldn't actually see him. It's quite frightening how blind I am. Still, that is another ambition fulfilled, to actually appear in a vampire film, to be part of that's story's made-up world, albeit fleetingly, so I'm quietly chuffed. Thank you Jason.

PRODUCTION

The film was shot over four weeks in early 2016, starting on January 18th and finishing on February 12th. Some extra scenes were shot on the evening of March 22nd and the *Jeunes* by Infinity advert two month later. There was even one final scene in which 18 was killed by Dexter shot later still, in October (you'll notice it differs from the book in which 18 gets away). These additional scenes helped shape the edit and improved the final film, although I still feel a tad sorry for 18.

All in all it's not a long time in which to shoot a film (*Wild Bill* had six weeks) and there were a few scenes that we weren't able to get simply because of the time constraints of a 20-day shoot. But all in all the cast and crew and Jason in particular performed miracles above and beyond the call of duty considering the conditions. The shoot came right in the middle of a cold snap when the temperatures rarely got above 0°C during the day. Then, when the sun went down in the evening, they would plunge into minus figures and a strange red haze would tint the frozen mists that hung over the set (my rear lights as I headed home).

Other than the temperature though, we were pretty lucky with the weather. It didn't snow, it only rained a couple of times and when it did we were able to film inside and no hurricanes rolled through Hertfordshire to halt production. That's important on a tight budget. A little luck is always needed and I'm relieved to say we had it on *Eat Local*. Otherwise it might not have got made. The day before the first day of filming it started snowing and I thought we were buggered. But the snows cleared overnight and never threatened again.

The same thing happened on *Wild Bill*. The first day of filming went swimmingly (and involved the scenes with Andy Serkis in the cemetery and train) but then the heavens opened on the second day. All the scenes that were scheduled to be shot that day had to be switched inside and a nearby cafe was bunged a couple of grand so that it could close for the day and let Dexter use it as an improvised location. In fact if you watch the cafe scene in which Bill, Terry and Dicky talk you can see it snowing outside. If it hadn't have been, this scene would've taken place at a bus stop (I think). It's better in a cafe though. I wish I'd thought of that.

No such problems on *Eat Local*. Other than the cold and a whole lot of mud, production was only threatened by the weather once, on the final Sunday when Eve and Billy filmed the scene in which Vanessa picks Sebastian up from the train station. The winds, the rain and the sleet were atrocious but they got what they needed and no one died in the process – at least no one important.

The main location used throughout the film was Stockers Farm. It's a working farm with stables and horses but also doubles as a film set and has appeared in a number of movies such as *28 Weeks Later* (the opening chase scenes with Robert Carlisle) and *Children of Men* (Michael Caine's house). It's a perfect film location. It looks like a rural idyll and could pass for anywhere – Sussex, Derbyshire or the Highlands – but it is in fact just inside the M25, 5mins from Rickmansworth High Street and within touching distance of The Groucho Club in Soho, an important factor when dealing with actors. In fact, it's just around the corner from a massive Tesco's, which provided many of the Ginsters wrappers that could be found in my car during the course of the shoot.

Stockers Farm.

The unit itself was based in a very nice pub on Woodcock Hill, Harefield Road called The Rose & Crown. This doubled as a location and the place where Mackenzie Crook and I locked acting horns and provided some of the soldiers' name to boot, with Private Rose (Nick Moran), Private Crown (Ben Starr) and Private Woodcock (me). Private Stoker (Dean Kember) was meant to be Private Stocker but I misspelled his name and no one thought to check, so these days I pretend I named him in honour of Bram Stoker, the father of all modern day vampires. But he wasn't. He was named in honour of my propensity for typos.

While we're on the subject, Simon Allix was named Private Putney because his scene was shot separately in March on Putney Common, just around the corner from another very nice pub, The Telegraph (see a pattern emerging?) and Nicolas Rowe was named Private Gary because he was meeting his mate Gary and couldn't stick around for a pint afterwards. Hardly scientific but you try and come up with half a dozen names at short notice and see how you do. Lastly, Rocci Williams was Private Frost for obvious weather-related reasons.

The other key location was Cholsey Railway Station in Oxfordshire. This acted as the location for Sebastian and Vanessa's first meeting place and our one and only scene with future superstars Kavab Stables and Roman Clark (aka. Mick and Nick). Give us a quid!

The catering was supplied (believe it or not) by Jamie Oliver. Yes, him off the telly. I never saw him frying any eggs in person but he provided all the equipment, the trucks, the food and the personnel in the shape Jai Harrower, Barnaby Benbow and Arron Harrower. More often that not you don't notice the crews' names at the end of a film but these guys are well worth pointing out, not only for the amazing grub they provided in difficult conditions but also for not owning a coat between them. In the middle of winter! On a night shoot! They did this fantastic Green curry one night that a posh Thai restaurant could've charged top dollar for and had everyone going back for seconds.

At least I went back for seconds. And I still managed a Ginsters on the way home. I am a writer not an actor. I can let myself go as much as I like.

Whatever happens with the film now, whether it cleans up at the Oscars or disappears without a trace, that's very much in the laps of the Gods. Either way, and purely from my own point of view, it was a wonderful experience to be a part of and something I'll never forget. Nor indeed will my son.

CHARLIE'S BIG DAY OUT

For most of my son's life, Charlie's only ever seen me slip off to the spare bedroom to tap on a keyboard. Most dads go to work (some even earn money apparently) but Charlie's dad just plays with the computer all day long while he's slogging his guts out at school. It must be hard for him to understand what I do. It's hard enough for me. So when *Eat Local* happened I decided to take Charlie along to the set to show him how films are made.

Who knows when I might get another chance?

First thing was first, I had to get him out of school. I sought permission from the Head teacher and dressed it up as work experience but she wasn't buying it. She said she couldn't authorise such an absence but agreed it sounded like a worthwhile experience. It would go down in Charlie's school record as an unauthorised absence but we wouldn't be fined.

Charlie reckoned he could live with that so one cloudy Wednesday in January, while his classmates went to school to sit up straight and stop mucking about, Charlie and me shared a massive bag of fizzy Haribos on our way to see the vampires at Stocker's Farm.

It was a lovely day. Freezing cold but fun. Charlie got to play with guns and rocket launchers and meet some of the cast and crew who were filming that day, all of whom made him feel very welcome. The only downside was that day's lunch. Mackerel. It's a fantastic fish and was done to perfection but it wasn't to Charlie's tastes so we shared a Ginsters and another bag of Haribos.

Here's some pictures I took from that day, one that I hope will live as long with Charlie as it will with me (now I just need to get three more films made in order to wangle my other kids a day off school).

Charlie and director, Jason Flemyng.

Two Charlies together; King and Cox (Henry).

With Billy Cook (Sebastian).

With Tony Curran (Boniface).

Charlie at the Coven's meeting table.

I'll give you "unauthorised absence".

Charlie in the Thatchers' fridge.

Filming on the hill.

Getting warm.

CAST

Henry	Charlie Cox
Angel	Freema Agyeman
Boniface	Tony Curran
Larousse	Mackenzie Crook
Colonel Bingham	Robert Portal
Vanessa	Eve Myles
Sebastian	Billy Cook
Alice	Annette Crosbie
Chen	Lukaz Leong
The Duke	Vince Regan
18	Johnny Palmiero
Mrs Thatcher	Ruth Jones
Mr Thatcher	Dexter Fletcher
Thomas	Jordan Long
Nick	Kavab Stables
Mick	Roman Clark
Mina	Elly Fairman
Lucy	Tine Stapelfeldt
Station Master	Blain Fairman
Private Putney	Simon Allix
Private Rose	Nick Moran
Private Crown	Ben Starr
Private Gary	Nicholas Rowe
Private Stoker	Dean Kember
Private Frost	Rocci Williams
Private Woodcock	Danny King
Soldiers	Adam Horton
	Adrian Bower
	Alan Eisner
	Alexander Sagar
	Andy Davies
	Andy Lister
	Asa Sims
	Ben Fairman
	Brian Court

190

Soldiers (cont.)_____Charles Albert
David Binnie
David Little
Gary Toms
George Craggs
Glen Steyn
Hue Wright
Jai Harrower
James Daniel Wilson
James Warren
Joseph Graggs
Judo Jim
Karl Foulkes
Kieran Clarke
Luke Osgrove
Milo Makromallis
Neil Webster
Oliver Leach
Paul Dickinson
Paul Storey
Philip Kemp
Sam Parham
Sergiy Kushayev
Stuart S-Garner
Ted Harrison
Will Sutton

CREW

Director_____Jason Flemyng
Producer_____Rod Smith
Producer_____Jonathan Sothcott
Line Producer_____Neil Jones
Production Manager_____Kat Stephens
Production Coordinator_____Aleisha McLardy
Production Designer_____Russell DeRozario
Editor_____Alex Fenn
First Assistant Director_____Mick Ward
Second Assistant Director_____Lee Tailor
Third Assistant Director_____Noel Corbally
Art Director_____Louise Vogel
Standby Art Director & Graphics_____Oskar DeRozario
Set Decorator_____Charlotte Taylor
Props Master_____George Morris
Construction Manager_____Danny Brown
Transport & Props_____Jimmy Edwards
Standby Armourer_____Rob Armitage
Cinematographer_____Chas Bain
Camera Operator/Steadicam_____Sean Savage
First Assistant Camera_____Simon Heck
Second Assistant_____Camera Scott Jamison
Camera Trainee_____Graeme McCormick
Tracking Quad Bike_____Matt Coulter
DIT_____Steve Evans
Costume Designer_____Sophie Canale
Costume Standby_____Nadia Merabti
Costume Advisor_____Sammy Sheldon
Costume Assistant_____Kasenya Dudley
Costume Standby_____Emma Evans
Costume Trainee_____Carolina Fernandaz

Post Production Supervisor_____Ian Grey
Production Sound Mixer_____John Hayes
First Assistant Sound_____Andrew Rowe
Second Assistant Sound_____Peter Allen
Composer_____James Brett
Supervisor Sound Editor_____Danny Sheehan
Post Production Audio_____Gavin Rose
Hair and Makeup Designer_____Tamara Ramsey-Crockett
Makeup Assistant_____Nancy Daniell
Makeup Trainee_____Sarah Wichall
Hair and Makeup Advisor_____Fae Hammond
Special Effects Makeup Designer_____Sangeet Prabhaker
Special Effects Makeup Trainee_____Dana Degan
Hairdresser_____Keith Beer
Make-up Trainee_____Daisy Beer
Prosthetics_____Chris Lyons
Script Supervisor_____Julia Chiavetta
Special Effects Supervisor_____David Payne
Special Effects Senior Technician_____Anthony Auger
Special Effects Senior Technician_____Karl Openshaw
Special Effects Senior Technician_____Jody Taylor
Special Effects Technician_____Alistair Anderson
Special Effects Technician_____Peter Simons
Stunt Coordinator_____Steve Dent
Stunt Rigger_____Will Dent
Bike Stunt Performer_____Kieran Clarke
Visual Effects Supervisor_____Theo Albanis
Visual Effects Supervisor_____Koutsoliotas Kostas
Gaffer_____Tom Gates
Best Boy/Electrician_____Adrian Mackay
Best Boy/Electrician_____Kevin Heathrington
Electrician_____Greg King
Electrician_____Camil Liberto
Electrician_____Niall Crawford
Electrician_____Paul Synnott
Electrician_____Ross Lusted
Electrician_____Terry Roberts
Electrician_____Tom Tailor

Key Grip_____Pat Garrett
Rigger_____John Fenelly
Rigging Consultant_____Sam Skipper
Fight Director (2nd Unit)_____Jason Statham
Stunt Action Camera (2nd Unit)_____Adam Horton
First Assistant Director (2nd Unit)_____Peter Freeman
Script Supervisor (2nd Unit)_____Sarah Armstrong
Third Assistant Director (2nd Unit)_____Faz Buffery
Casting Director_____Lucinda Syson
Assisting Casting Director_____Bex Reynolds
Casting Associate_____Natasha Vincent
Head of Marketing_____Amanda Kerridge
Unit Publicist_____Adam Stephen Kelly
EPK/Stills Photographer_____Joe de Kadt
Artwork_____Mike Kus
Medic_____Cheryl Ellen
Head Caterer_____Jai Harrower
Caterer_____Barnaby Benbow
Caterer_____Arron Harrower
Production Accountant_____Shayne Savill
Key Floor Runner_____Jack Fontaine
Production Runner/Driver_____Theodore Hammond
Production Runner/Driver_____Sophie Yauner
Production Runner/Driver_____Charlotte Carey
Production Runner/Driver_____Angelos Talentzakis
Production Runner/Driver_____Kieran Hayhow
Production Runner/Driver_____Dennis Boon
Production Runner/Driver_____Harpal Deol
Trainee Production Runner_____Marli Hart
Location/Unit Manager_____John Curtis
Location Assistant_____Richard Orr
Security Guard_____Jerry-Lee Mackenzie
Security Guard_____Mariuse Bednore
Driver_____Lol Smith
Driver_____Denis Gilmore
Driver_____Duncan Bradley
Writer_____Danny King

BIOGRAPHY

Danny King has written for the page, stage, big and small screens. Born in Slough in 1969, he excelled at underachieving, leaving school with no qualifications to work as a hod carrier throughout the late 1980s housing boom. A couple of brushes with the law forced him to sit up and think, so he enlisted in an Access Course and went on to study journalism at The London College of Printing. He spent the next ten years in the magazine industry on such terrible titles as *Model Railway Enthusiast* and *Stamp Magazine* before rising (or sinking, depending on your point of view) to become the Editor of Paul Raymond's flagship title, *Mayfair*. His first book, *The Burglar Diaries*, was published in 2001 to critical acclaim and became the basis of his BBC Three sitcom, *Thieves Like Us*. Eight more novels followed, together with his debut feature, *Wild Bill*, for which he and co-writer Dexter Fletcher won a Writers' Guild of Great Britain award and a BAFTA nomination. He lives in Chichester, West Sussex with his wife Jeannie and four children and is rarely seen out during the hours of daylight.

Lightning Source UK Ltd.
Milton Keynes UK
UKOW06f1143040917
308549UK00007B/66/P